Michèle Roberts is the author of eleven novels including *Daughters of the House* (1992) which won the WH Smith Literary Award and was shortlisted for the Booker Prize. She has also published another volume of short stories, *During Mother's Absence*, and has recently collected her poetry in *In All the Selves I Was*. Half-English and half-French, Michèle Roberts lives in London and in the Mayenne, France.

PLAYING
SARDINES

Michèle Roberts

Virago

A *Virago* Book

First published by Virago Press 2001
This edition published 2002
Reprinted 2003 (twice)

Copyright © Michèle Roberts 2001

The moral right of the author has been asserted

A CIP catalogue record for this book
is available from the British Library

ISBN 1 86049 935 X

Typeset in Garamond by M Rules
Printed and bound in Great Britain by
Clays Ltd, St Ives plc

Virago Press
An imprint of
Time Warner Books UK
Brettenham House
Lancaster Place
London WC2E 7EN

www.virago.co.uk

In memoriam Lorna Sage

ACKNOWLEDGEMENTS

Some of these stories were commissioned and written for BBC Radio 3 and Radio 4. Some of the other stories first appeared in the following magazines or anthologies: *Obsessions, Reshape Whilst Damp,* the *Mail on Sunday* magazine, *Sex Drugs Rock'n'Roll, The Time Out Book of Paris Short Stories, The Time Out Book of London Short Stories, Woman and Home,* the *Sunday Express* magazine, and *Ovid Revisited.* My thanks to all the editors involved. All these stories have been rewritten for inclusion here.

Thanks to Lennie Goodings and all at Little, Brown/Virago, and to Gillon Aitken and all at Gillon Aitken Associates. Thanks to all my friends.

CONTENTS

PLAYING SARDINES

for Lorna Sage

I bought the tin of sardines in Borough market, the gourmet-food version held on the site of the ordinary fruit and veg one on the third Saturday of every month. Portuguese sardines, that I picked out from the surrounding jars of ground pimento, heaps of chorizos, and plump-hipped bottles of white wine scrambled together on the lace-covered trestle table. I chose them simply because the tin they came in was foreign and beautiful: not oblong but oval, labelled in scarlet and yellow, with swirly blue lettering in Portuguese and a picture of a booted and sou'westered fisherman holding up a monster fish by its tail.

The food sold in that market is all organic, farm-fresh, hand-reared and so forth, to show you what can be done if you take your eyes off the supermarket shelves for a second, but it is expensive. The pleasure of wandering between the stalls resides mainly in looking and marvelling. You don't assume you're going to buy anything, necessarily, though you accept all the free tastes you're offered, shavings of Wensleydale or curls of honey-crackled ham. You hover over trays of smoked trout, imagine clotted cream and apricot jam sliding down your throat. You buy the Welsh goats' cheeses, boxes of lamb's lettuce from Herefordshire, and flasks of Somerset cider vinegar as occasional Sunday treats, or as birthday presents for your friends.

Just looking at the food was enough, enjoying the prodigality and variety of what was on offer. It felt quite in order to select the sardines solely for the sake of their gaily-coloured tin and take them home to display on the kitchen shelf next to the packet of couscous illustrated by a palm tree and strip of beach, the two little pots of harissa flourishing red and green parrots, the Camembert boxes showing buxom farm-maids in flowery meadows tending to their cows, and the squat can of Spanish olive oil decorated with gold arabesques.

My appreciation of pretty packaging went back to when I was young, and wanted real paintings on my walls but could not afford them, and did not dare assume I could paint them myself. I used to pick up scrap wooden fruit trays and cardboard boxes chucked down by the Saturday traders in Portobello Road, selecting the ones whose labels and stencilled lettering I liked best, cart them home to the damp cold-water flat I was illegally subletting in Powys Square from a housing-association tenant, reduce them down to single flat panels, and nail them up. They had been carefully designed, printed and put together, and I wanted to save them from going to waste. I cherished their beauty. They did not deserve to be thrown away.

Likewise, one summer in Venice, when I was still young, and foolish too, I collected screwed-up and discarded orange-wrappers from behind the fruit stalls where they were cast along with the cabbage stalks and bruised plums rolling in confusion with all the other fascinating litter of coarse lettuce leaves and broken, juice-stained redcurrant punnets and rotten courgettes, until the corporation-men swept this booty into the rubbish-barge, or the nuns, scavenging indiscriminately for their soup-kitchens, scooped it up into their big wicker baskets, whoever got there first.

In those days Italian oranges were jacketed in pale yellow tissue paper stamped with charming designs in two or three colours. Adam and Eve disported themselves among stags and unicorns; satyrs blew trumpets; volcanoes erupted; suns blazed among the stars. Uncrumpled, wrinkles patiently smoothed away with a fingertip, so that the delicate paper did not tear, flattened out back into the original gold-rimmed squares, then carefully ironed, the little sheets of pictures could subsequently be framed and packed in my suitcase. I couldn't hang them up in the Contessa's low-ceilinged but chic garret. She would have thought they were out of place.

I had married an architectural historian at rather short notice two months previously, after he had taken me to visit Italy for the first time, and had accompanied him back out to Venice, where he was compiling a catalogue of architectural drawings for a forthcoming exhibition. As a result of visiting so many famous villas and writing about their porticos, or their vaulting, or their colonnades, he had many grand acquaintances, which is why we were renting the attic flat at the top of the Contessa's tall house in a

narrow *calle* off the piazza of Santa Maria del Giglio, near San
Marco. The architectural historian had a distinguished appearance; also he wore jackets of the finest herringbone tweed, trousers
of the finest wool. All the lonely, bored contessas whose *palazzi* he
visited loved the way he listened to them so intently, his head on
one side and his fingertips pressed together. They invited him frequently to dinner and ran him about in their cars and lent him
their summer houses on Capri.

To save him money during the four-months trip, because I did
not have a job out here and we were living on his salary and travel
and research grants, we never went out to restaurants. I cooked at
home. Twice a week a few fruit and vegetable stalls set up in the
piazza under striped blue and white awnings, and on those days I
was able to do some of the shopping here, sparing myself a long
walk back from the big Rialto market lugging heavy bags of food,
wine and water, which had then to be humped up five flights of
slippery marble stairs. It was the season of the aftermath of the
Chernobyl disaster. *Carabinieri* patrolled the street markets enfor-
cing the putting-up of posters warning the populace to be careful
what they ate, but I bought oranges and picked up the orange-
wrappers regardless. They were too appealing to waste.

I was a collector of *art brut* in self-defence. I needed a tiny
space of esoteric information that was exclusively mine, in order
not to feel crushed by my inadequacies. The architectural historian
was a renowned expert on the theory and practice of Renaissance
building. When he took me out sightseeing he would linger for
hours in cold churches (Renaissance churches only – I was dis-
couraged from admiring the medieval or the baroque) in order to

make ground-breaking discoveries: that a particular tomb might have been designed by Sansovino; that the style of a particular capital matched the details of one in a drawing by Palladio. Then he would disappear for days into the state archive near San Rocco to unearth the supporting documents.

In the face of this intimidating sharp-eyed expertise, I hastily learned to appreciate Renaissance notions of the beautiful, based on order, harmony and proportion, and to know my cornices from my architraves. At the same time I refined my connoisseurship as a collector of rubbish. I walked through Venice with my gaze swivelling down as well as round and up: I could spot an interesting brown-paper bag, patterned with motifs of meringues and brioches, discarded outside a *pasticceria*, at twenty paces; I could penetrate at a single glance the bulky sacks of refuse toppling on the side of the *fondamenta* outside houses that were being done up, and know instantly whether or not it was worth sneaking back later to rootle through them for fragments of old tile or scraps of carved and gilded wood.

After two months in Venice, I had absorbed so much information about different ways of turning corners with pilasters, or methods of tucking farm buildings behind the wings of villas, that I was a less amusing companion than I'd been at the beginning of our marriage. My initial patina of naïve charm was wearing off. So new women, desperate to learn about architecture, began popping up, like capitals and tombs, each one more intriguing and appealing than her predecessor, in the archive, the university library, the *superintendenza*'s office, or simply in the bar where my husband drank his morning cappuccino, and he felt obliged to pursue each fresh and delicious object of desire with all the single-minded passion of which a true scholar is capable. Long visits to churches would ensue. Then he'd return to our garret flat for lunch, accompanied by the latest wounded bird, who needed the friendship of a strong woman like me.

I might have been strong but I was also unsatisfactory. I walked around the flat barefoot; I didn't bother wearing makeup because it melted off in the heat; I drank more wine than a decorous *signora* should; my clothes were not elegant; and I had been caught mopping up the sauce on my plate with a piece of bread stuck on the end of my fork. If you had to mop, my husband explained, then fingers were better than forks. But it was better not to mop at all, certainly at dinner parties, and it was also better not so often to accept second helpings.

It was in Italy that I first ate fresh sardines. Before that, in England, they'd come in tins, oblong ones, complete with keys. The key had a slit in its tail which corresponded with a flap of metal welded on to the underneath of the tin, at one end. You inserted metal tongue into key slit, gave the key one quick initial twist, flipping the tongue to bend over, the parts to catch and fit, until they gripped well together, without sliding away separate again; and then to unpeel the lid you turned the key, travelling it across from one ridged silvery end to the other, rolling up a long section of tin as you went. The opener cut along parallel to the tin's edge, most pleasingly, as your fingers worked it. The dangerously sharp-edged strip of metal finished up wound neatly on to your little implement, and the opened rectangular gap revealed the sardines, blackish blocks minus heads and tails, intimately packed in together under a quilt of oil. You ate them mashed on buttered toast, having first lifted out, on a knife-tip, their stretches of knuckled spine like decayed zips.

Often, however, the key slipped on the tin's tongue half-way and its mouth refused fully to open, or the key would not engage, or got stuck, or broke off before you'd even properly begun, and then the frustration was extreme, and all you could do, grumpy and hungry, was hurl the tin away into the rubbish.

Fresh sardines I discovered at a neo-Palladian villa in the Veneto. We had been invited for dinner so that my husband could inspect our host's archive, in his pursuit of certain sixteenth-century documents relating to an attribution he was currently working on, and also the fine collection of antiquarian books that had been built up by the family over the centuries. Our aristocratic patron, who was related to our landlady in Venice, was an elderly bachelor who lived alone. Most of the villa was shut up, he explained on the telephone, to save money on heating, but nonetheless we were very welcome and he would do his best to give us something half-way decent to eat. We were to take the little local train, and then a taxi from the village, which he would order for us, and he would expect us at seven o'clock.

I had by now visited most of Palladio's villas, even the ones not open to the public. Some were lived in by rich people, and had been sumptuously restored; others got by as best they might. One, for example, was currently a lamp and striplight shop jostled by the factories and bleak housing of an industrial zone, its farm and gardens long gone; another, encroached on by rolling fields of towering maize, was furnished with nothing but iron bedsteads in its shabby, vast rooms, and had chickens pecking about over its tessellated floors. Our host's villa, having been built fifty years too late, and being somewhat over-ornate, lacked the austere grace of the true, original Palladian style, and so my husband did not bother hovering about too long outside admiring its façade. He contented himself with pointing out the number of columns cluttering up the loggia on the top storey, and the slightly awkward sweep of the stable block.

Our host turned out to live in the right-hand wing, opposite the stables, in a lofty-ceilinged and frescoed interior which was stuffed with decaying antique furniture and gloomily lit by gilt chandeliers. In between the painted panels hung worn tapestries and the heads of dead animals. On arrival we had deposited our coats in a marble-floored vestibule off the imposing circular entrance hall, and now we followed the young black-haired retainer, dressed in a peculiar, tight-fitting brown jacket, who had opened the door to us, through three interconnecting saloons, each one darker and chillier than the last.

Our host was finally run to earth in a shadowy drawing-room, whose shutters, he explained, were kept closed to stop the sun fading the carpets by day and the mosquitoes entering by night. He was a small man wearing brown shoes that gleamed in the twilight. Like my husband, he was faultlessly dressed in an immaculately cut suit. He kissed my hand, pretending not to notice the short black denim skirt and long-sleeved striped Breton T-shirt I was wearing, which had caused my husband such grief five minutes ago when he realized what I had on under my raincoat.

– A very simple dinner, our host warned us: you'll have to understand, an old bachelor like me, I'm not used to entertaining. I hope you'll make allowances for the primitive fare I'll be offering you.

We were not the only guests. In my husband's honour our host had also invited the director of the local museum, and one of his curators, who specialized in Renaissance ivories and faience. She was slender, and very smartly dressed in a calf-length pleated green silk dress with silver and diamanté buttons. Her nails were painted pale pink, her hair subtly blonded and swept up in a chignon, her face expertly made up. Her feet were expensively shod in crocodile. She had a sweet, vulnerable look, and I saw my husband spot this and smile encouragingly at her.

The introductions made, the sips of *prosecco* taken, the Japanese crackers nibbled, we were ushered through double doors into the dining-room. The table bristled with elaborate settings: arrays of cut-glass goblets and frilly-edged white porcelain plates, ranks of silver cutlery, two tall candelabra, and mounds of enormous starched white napkins. How sensible these were: you could wrap them around yourself, like the towels hairdressers swathed you in before they brandished the scissors, and then you did not splash embarrassing drips of *pastaciutta* sauce down your chin or front. I lifted and shook out my vast linen bib and tucked it into the neck of my T-shirt. I hastily untucked it again, lowered it, and smoothed it over my lap, as all the others were doing, as soon as I saw my husband glare at me. I glared back, and he turned his head and began to talk to the well-groomed blonde lady, who was sitting next to him.

I cheered up when I was given a small glass of pale gold wine. A white-gloved hand came from behind me and poured from a decanter. I had not seen white gloves since my convent-school days. I twisted round in my delicate eighteenth-century dining-chair and glanced at the owner of the hand. I had never seen a man in white gloves in my entire life. This one was the young retainer with curly black hair who had shown us in earlier. He still wore his tightly buttoned brown jacket, that I now saw simulated a livery of some kind, but to serve the dinner he had added the white gloves and a white cloth folded over one arm. He smiled at me as he tilted out the wine without spilling a single drop, then twisted his wrist and spun the decanter away.

Dinner began with *pappardelle* in hare sauce, the wide noodles delicate and light as could be. I was impressed with our host's skill. Next came the sardines, much longer and fatter than they looked when tinned, resplendent and blackly shining on a big antique majolica plate. I speculated as to whether our host had a special fondness for the south, for he had cooked the sardines *alla siciliana*, stuffed with chopped sultanas, anchovies, black olives, and garlic, a sliver or two of lemon peel, and some minced parsley, a *soupçon* of mint. They had been brushed with olive oil and then grilled. I ate my portion of delicious scented fish as slowly as possible, trying to work out the recipe, wondering whether it was the same as the one given in Alda Boni's compendium *Il Talismano della Felicità*.

I used to read this cookery book at night, after my husband had fallen asleep, savouring its poetry, its precise vocabulary. Recipes were indeed like poems, compact with carefully chosen words.

You were supposed not to overdo it, not to stuff in too many words, too many ingredients. Subtlety and finesse mattered; you left out anything that wasn't strictly necessary. Change the ingredients, just a couple, and one regional dish slipped into the version made in the village next door, the village on the other side of the hill.

There were various ways, for example, of making lamb stew with white haricot beans, tomatoes, and white wine; it all depended on which part of Tuscany your mother had come from, what the source of her particular recipe was, and whether or not she included rosemary. Italian cooking was not indiscriminate: you never threw black pepper into your *ragù* just because you felt like it; you included it only if the recipe traditionally called for it. I, who had prided myself in my art-school days on my Bolognese sauce made with whatever I could find in the cupboard, now learned to simmer the best beef and tomatoes and onions with good red wine and proper meat stock, to adjust its fragrance with a clove or two, some salt but no black pepper or garlic, to finish it, after a couple of hours, with a ladleful of cream, and never, under any circumstances whatsoever, to let the green peppers so beloved of student cooks in the early seventies anywhere near it.

These musings got me through the rest of the excellent and elaborate dinner over whose preparation our host must have toiled all day. Boiled meats with *mostarda* pickles, then a green salad of mixed wild leaves spiced with rocket, then cheese, and finally cold caramelized rice cake flavoured with nutmeg, lemon and cinnamon.

I couldn't have drunk too much even if I'd tried. The decanter appeared briefly with each successive dish, then vanished. Half a small glass of wine at the beginning of each course, for me, served by the smiling footman, and one glass apiece, lasting the whole of dinner, for my four companions. They did not discuss what they ate, which would have been, I had learned by now, bad manners; they were embroiled in a passionate and complex discussion of architecture that I couldn't join in. My Italian was not yet good enough.

Quite soon, in any case, my husband shifted his exclusive attention to the blonde *signorina*. He bent his head towards her and looked at her from under his eyelashes. He listened very attentively to her as she spoke, as though they were the only two people in the whole of creation. She appeared to be telling him all about the villa's beautiful gardens, and the shell-studded eighteenth-century grotto which had recently been opened up at their far end. Completely out of my husband's period, of course, which was why our host had been too modest to mention it. My husband murmured excitedly and intimately. The *signorina* glanced at him shyly. As soon as we had finished our coffee, served in tiny espresso cups, he led her from the room, explaining gaily over his shoulder that he simply had to go and see the grotto before it grew too dark to appreciate it properly.

The rest of us lingered on at table, drinking more coffee, then toying with thimbles of *grappa* and *amaro*. Half an hour passed. I made stilted conversation about the beauties of Venetian painting and architecture. Fired, finally, by the *grappa*, which I knew ladies were not supposed to drink, I expatiated on the talents of Tiepolo and Titian, the purity of Palladio, the sensitive severity of Sansovino. My two companions, somewhat embarrassed by my eloquence, let alone by my husband's prolonged absence from the party, began yawning discreetly and glancing at their watches. The last train back to Venice left quite early, and we had not yet been shown the library and our host's collection of incunabula, which was supposedly the whole purpose of our visit.

I got up and excused myself, muttering something about wanting to go and admire the stables. My host stood up and bowed, waved a courteous hand.

Please. Wander wherever you like. We shall go and begin to look at the books in the library.

I wanted the lavatory, but was too timid to ask for it. I presumed it was one of those words not spoken in polite dining-rooms. I hurried out, and circled the suite of saloons several times, avoiding the now-empty dining-room and what I guessed must be the library, backing away every time I approached the tall, double wooden doors and heard the men's voices behind. I looped back and forth, constantly returning to the circular entrance hall. Six sets of doors opened off it. It was just a question of choosing correctly. All the doors looked identically handsome, rather forbidding; you couldn't tell what was concealed behind them.

I caught a whiff of sardine and turned round to peer into a dark corner behind the wide stone staircase. Ahead of me was a single, narrow door which I guessed might give on to the kitchen. I pushed it open, went down a short corridor, opened another door, and entered a cave of heat and commotion.

In here the blackened, vaulted walls were hung with copper pans and cake moulds like big rosy-gold blooms. A radio babbled in one corner. Around a wide old sink thronged at least half a dozen aproned women. They were busy washing up amidst clouds of steam, clattering dishes and saucepans, all energetically talking at once in deep contralto voices as they scoured and wiped.

The kitchen opera ceased as I came in. The women all spun round and looked at me in a considering way. They showed no surprise at my abrupt entry. They seemed to have comprehended immediately that I was one of the dinner guests. Now, their affable faces told me, I was their guest also, and they were waiting to see how they could offer me hospitality.

– *Mi dispiace di disturbarvi . . . ma . . . il gabinetto, per favore?* I tried: WC?

The young footman with curly black hair had thrown his brown jacket over the back of his wooden chair. He was wearing a white, short-sleeved T-shirt. When he pushed away his empty plate and sprang up from the table, I saw that he was wearing jeans, and sneakers just like mine. The large flat dish in front of him held a second lot of sardines, a discreet orgy of fish beautifully arranged head to tail, their shining silver-black skins scattered with parsley and garnished with slices of lemon.

Now I realized that it was of course this team of sturdy women, presumably recruited from the local village, who had spent their time preparing and cooking all the delicacies we had eaten earlier on, not our host with his manicured politeness and his trousers falling in exquisite pleats over his well-polished shoes. How foolish I was not to have understood sooner.

I fished up my best Italian. I thanked the smiling ladies for dinner. I complimented them clumsily but sincerely on the excellence of their cooking, particularly on their way with sardines. I apologized for disturbing their supper.

They exclaimed and scoffed at this. They were not yet ready to sit down and eat, not until they had finished all the clearing-up. In the meantime, Federico could show me to where I needed to go. They waved me off and turned back to their work.

The young man, armed by the cooks with a basket containing a clean towel, a bar of soap, and a bottle of eau-de-Cologne, escorted me up two flights of stairs without fuss. He opened a door and arranged the contents of his basket on the washstand within, made sure there was a brush and comb to hand, and showed me how to flush the antique cistern. He closed the door, waited for me to emerge, then showed me downstairs again. Our sneakers squeaked on the stone steps as we trampled past the masks of foxes and hares.

In the hall he paused. He spoke slowly so that I would understand.

– Would you like a cigarette?

We went out through a small side door into pitch blackness. I stumbled, and Federico caught my arm. He steered me over cobbles, round a corner. Now a lantern gleamed from its hook on a post, and we were approaching the kitchen from the yard. Under the lighted window a bench stood on the gravel, flanked by pots of bay and flowering oleander. The pale blossoms glimmered in the darkness. The air was warm on my neck and face. It smelt aromatic, as though cedars grew nearby.

We sat in silence for a while, smoking the ferocious cigarettes Federico produced from his jeans pocket. Then he pointed towards the low wall of the yard, the semi-invisible garden beyond.

– That's the terrace, over there, you can just see the statues along the balustrade, and below that the steps leading to the cypress walk. Your husband is down there somewhere, with the blonde lady.

– I know, I said.

Federico shrugged.

I didn't know how to explain I had stopped minding. Instead I asked Federico if he was related to the women in the kitchen.

– My mother, he said: and her sisters-in-law. My aunts by marriage.

His father's family, he told me, was from the south. Life being so difficult down there, his father had come north to find work, as a young man, had married a northern girl, had stayed. So Federico's mother had learned to cook certain southern dishes, to remind her husband of home. Like the stuffed and grilled sardines, which had become one of her specialities, and which were now a favourite with our host.

My marriage had been a version of coming north, I thought. My husband had seemed so glamorous at first.

I felt like crying, and took a deep drag on my cigarette, to stop myself.

– I thought I'd fallen in love with my husband, I said to Federico: but of course it was Italy I'd really fallen in love with, not him at all.

I thought I'd better change the subject, in case I did indeed start crying.

– In England, I said: in my childhood, we used to play a game called sardines.

I wished I could speak Italian well enough to describe it, as a way of trying to thank him for his company, and for the cigarettes. I wanted to convey how the house was plunged into darkness and so transformed into a mysterious new landscape, how the point of the game was hiding yourself, in an impossible place no one normally ever went to or would ever dream of finding you in, and then waiting for someone to discover you. Of course you hoped it would be the person you loved the most, the person in whose presence you were speechless and clumsy and weak at the knees. You dreamed how he would approach you in the darkness, unsure whether you were really there or not, how he would stand still, and listen for your breathing, sniffing you, but not touching you, and the air between your skin and his would grow warm then ignite with your longing. Perhaps, still saying nothing, he would stretch out a hand and trace with his finger the outline of your face and guess your identity. Perhaps you would kiss and caress each other, your hands plunging under the layers of your clothes to find the warm reality underneath. Then, if you were unlucky, all too soon, one by one, the others would find you, and pile in, giggling and whispering, which was when the game became truly sardines. But the best was to be the first two sardines alone in the dark and not speaking and just beginning to dare to touch.

We smoked a final cigarette and then Federico went back to the kitchen, and to his supper, and I returned to the library and to the incunabula session. Afterwards the blonde lady drove us back to the village just in time for us to catch the last train back to Venice.

Shortly afterwards I returned to London and to the single life. I was penniless and homeless all over again, but at least my suitcase was full of *art brut*, cookery books and drawings, and my imagination crammed with ideas for all the paintings I wanted to make. Prowling Portobello Road once more, on the lookout for interesting junk, I was intrigued to perceive how the neo-classical architecture of the Notting Hill streets sprang freshly alive at me now that I knew the names of all the different parts of the houses and could recite those classifications, that poetry.

MONSIEUR MALLARMÉ
CHANGES NAMES

for Paul Quinn

Until lack of inspiration threatened him with despair and disaster at the very peak of his career, Monsieur Mallarmé was a happy man. He was a poet. For many years he wrote prolifically and with increasing renown. He spent his days shifting words around, up and down, to and fro, from one line to another; he was obsessed with moving their places about on the page; he was constantly tossing them up and down in the palm of his hand like jacks or dice. He rearranged them like red and blue and purple anemones de Caen in a vase or *mâche* and *pissenlit* salad leaves on a plate. He wrote them down on pieces of paper which he then tore up and threw out of the window so that he could watch the fragments whirl off over the boulevards; proper *flâneurs*. He dreamed of a page in perpetual motion, a scribing machine which would compose poems whose order of words changed frequently according to a secret prearranged rhythm so that the poem would be different on each reading and no one could claim to recognize the realest or truest version. Poems were like white swans beating their wings and they were like white marble tombstones tenderly memorializing dead friends. The images for poems, let alone the poems themselves, danced about on his tongue and spilled down on to any writing surface that presented itself: his shirt cuff, his table napkin, the inside of his wife's wrist, which he would suddenly seize and inscribe with the invisible ink of his fingertip during a walk in the forest of Fontainebleau.

Their summer house was at Valvins, just outside Paris. It perched on the very edge of the Seine, which flowed past the bottom of their garden. The forest bristled on the far shore. When Mallarmé wasn't strolling along its green alleys, he was tacking up and down the broad river in his small sailing-boat. His wife and daughter, wearing loose linen clothes and straw hats, sat in the garden in basket-chairs, reading and sewing, or they weeded the flowerbeds surrounding the gravelled walks of espaliered apples that criss-crossed the grass. Friends arrived from the city to visit on Sundays, and were given lunch outside at a table set in the shade, spread with a white cloth, and adorned with jugs of roses. They ate crudités of radishes and shaved carrots and celery from the *potager*, roast chicken, and patisserie. Vuillard came, and Manet and Degas. Once out here in the countryside, they felt off-duty, and could relax. There was a kind of mental unbuttoning of shirt collars and loosening of ties that went on. They could play bowls and croquet, eat as many redcurrant tarts as they wanted, go for a sail in the little boat, smoke endless cigarettes, flirt gently with the Mallarmé ladies, and sprawl at ease in the sunshine sipping coffee and liqueurs.

When they visited the Mallarmés in Paris, at their third-floor flat in the rue de Rome, it was a much more formal affair. Mallarmé was conscious of being the most famous and respected poet of his day, of having a reputation for genius to live up to. He was a kind of unofficial laureate – the prince of poets, elected by his peers – and took his responsibilities fervently. He received his guests at his regular Tuesday-evening salon, after dinner, a ritual event which became famous for the high seriousness of the discourse on offer, the fragrant crowdedness of the little dining-room packed with men smoking pipes and cigars, and the excellence of the hot lemon-flavoured rum punch spiked with cloves. Mallarmé would lean against the marble mantelpiece and deliver disquisitions on literature and art and everybody felt obliged to be really intelligent and well-informed on the latest cultural issues of the day in case they were asked to comment. Whereas weekending in Valvins they could be childish if they wanted; they could lie on their backs on the grass; they could doze off and say nothing at all; or they could crack risqué jokes and tell bawdy stories; they could feel peacefully and comfortably themselves. At Valvins they were not required to ponder the nature of linguistic symbols or the relationship between music and painting, or to discuss the role of the omniscient narrator in the modern novel. The decisions that had to be made were of a less elevated order: whether to allow oneself another glass of *vin blanc cassis*; whether to suggest a piano duet to Madame Mallarmé; whether to go fishing. The painters often worked while they were down, and this for them was of course a form of pleasure. Vuillard, for example, produced three small oils of the house seen from the garden, while Degas made sketches of his hostess peeling vegetables and doing the ironing. Everyone understood that if Mallarmé needed to get on with some writing, he would slip away to his study upstairs and no one would mind. During his absences they were very well entertained by the two ladies of the household, the pretty mother and her beautiful daughter.

The house was small, shoebox-shaped, buried in its leafy, hedged garden brimming with flowering creepers and arches of roses. Downstairs were the damp kitchen, and the cellars smelling of wine and earth, upstairs the dining-room and a couple of bed-rooms, one for the two women, and the other for Mallarmé. His bed stood in one corner, and his desk under the window looking out over the Seine. A small glass-fronted bookcase held his collec-tion of works in English. He was fond of the works of Edgar Allan Poe and the detective stories of Sir Arthur Conan Doyle. One door connected to the dining-room, and another to the tiny land-ing and thence to his wife and daughter's room, with its shared bed and chest and washstand. He had a rocking-chair, brought back from his trip to London years before, set in front of the small fire-place, and here he would sit, pipe in mouth and papers on knee, writing, crossing out, rewriting, cancelling, until summoned for dinner or lunch.

The Mallarmé family spent two or three months at Valvins every year. Mallarmé would run up to town now and then to visit his great friend Madame Méry Laurent, the celebrated actress who was now retired from the stage but not from any of her enjoyments. In her day she had been a famous beauty, and in Stephane Mallarmé's eyes she still was. She was as tall and ample-bodied as he, with curly hair of undiminished gold, and almond-shaped grey eyes. They would eat luncheon together in her opulent apartment, sitting side by side on carved chairs at a massive table under a lampshade ballooning as pink and frilly as Méry's underskirts, sipping icy champagne while a maid served them with *pâté de foie gras* or oysters or lobster or *petits pois à la crème*, depending on the exact moment in the season and the whim of Méry's cook. After spending the afternoon in bed together they would drive in the Bois or stroll in the Luxembourg gardens, ending up at a favourite café to meet friends for gossip and drinks.

The latest craze among the painters was the new science of photography. Degas, for example, made portraits of all his inti-mates, including one of Stephane and Méry dressed up in Auvergnat peasant costumes, holding walking-sticks, posed against a backdrop of crags and waterfalls. Mallarmé was fascinated by the technique required for developing the image on the photographic plate, which he compared to the swimming-up of a poem into consciousness.

He had not been able to realize the invention he dreamed of, the page which would keep moving, endlessly re-forming the poem into different shapes. He was suddenly sick of writing mys-terious and perfect sonnets. But he was stuck, as fixed as any page in any book folded and gathered and stitched. He could not see how to move forward, how to discover and reach his next goal. To outsiders his life appeared enviably easy and trouble-free, even luxurious: he had a flat in Paris and a country retreat in Valvins, a small private income and hence no money worries, a devoted wife and daughter, an affectionate and accomplished mistress, several good close friends, a host of admirers and disciples, a sailing-boat; he could afford good wine and food and tobacco; he was in robust health.

The only problem was that he could no longer write poetry, did not know what to write or how to write, did not even want to write.

He said to Méry: I'm a failure. I'm finished.

He was lying in her bed in her flat just down the street from his own in the rue de Rome, lolling apparently very much at his ease, propped on a heap of lace-edged pillows, the apricot silk sheets rumpled around his naked chest, one arm flung up behind his head, one hand holding a cigar. An open bottle of champagne stood on the night-table, which was draped with a fringed gypsy shawl in pink and green silk. Above the bed a domed baldaquin unloosed falls of golden brocade which poured down around the hills of pillows and cushions and were looped back with strings of large fake pearls.

The bed was very much Méry's stage. It was where she displayed her talent for seduction, occasionally hammed up, to amuse him, with flashing eyes and tossed-back hair; it was where she made her nightly appearance, magnificently nude apart from her makeup and her amber earrings; it was where she acted out her devotion to her *cher* Stephane and recited charming speeches of passion; it was where she played the coquette, the soubrette, the midinette, but never the tragic heroine; where when she felt it

necessary to rescue a weak performance she produced clever sim-
ulations of ecstasy; where she danced for Mallarmé, sang to him,
dandled him, told him stories, did strip-tease, made him laugh,
and generally convinced him that while he was in it, this bed was
the very centre of the universe.

He sprawled, sighing, watching her get dressed. The golden
sunlight of late afternoon slipped under the lowered blinds and
patched the yellow carpet. It caressed Méry's blonde hair and
glowed on her shoulders and back as she bent to pull up her
stockings.

— Being a failure's just another pose, she answered him: you'll
have to work at it.

She twitched her garters into place and tied them. They were
sewn with forget-me-nots. He had bought them for her himself as
a present the day before. Watching her fingers briefly pat the blue
cotton flowers, he remembered how he had taken the garters out
of their tissue-paper-lined box and played with them, tested them
on his fingers, admiring, amused at the delight you could take in
such fripperies, the seriousness with which you discriminated
between these ones of rolled violet silk and these others decorated
with tiny knots of black lace. She had taught him how to buy such
gifts for her and he had discovered he enjoyed going with her to
choose the required frivolous accessories in a warm, perfumed
shop, attended by smart, well made-up young women, watching
her try on gloves, flourish and twist her wrist and hesitate between
lemon kid and sky-blue; he was an amused spectator as she
dithered over ankle boots buttoned to the side or the front, over
evening slippers with diamanté on the heels or without. It didn't

really matter if you didn't get it right, or if you changed your mind, because the following day you could go out and purchase another pair in quite another cut or colour. It wasn't solely a question of money. Méry, had she had no money whatsoever to spend on adorning herself, would still have deliberated with equal seriousness over whether to arrange dandelions, picked from a bit of wasteland in Montmartre, in the same glass as buttercups or daisies; whether to drink her morning cup of coffee in bed or by the window; whether to whistle in the bath or to sing. Her days were rich with small decisions and she arranged and rearranged her world with skill, choosiness and satisfaction. She was an artist of life; she composed it and recomposed it, played with it and let it change into something else every day.

– The trouble with you, Méry said: is that . . .

Her voice tailed dreamily off as she surveyed her reflection in the mirror. Mallarmé, watching her pull on her drawers and pick up her stays, realized that his problem could be solved. To celebrate he took her out to the café Procope for dinner. That night he concentrated on giving her pleasure, realizing how often it was the other way around.

He returned to Valvins by the first morning train, carrying a bulging overnight bag and greeting his wife and daughter with fond kisses. After lunch, he volunteered, for the first time ever in his life, to do the washing-up. Madame and Mademoiselle Mallarmé assumed he had heatstroke and gazed at him with concern. When he insisted, they went off, whispering to each other, into the radiant garden, while he juggled knives and forks into jugs of soapy water, piled plates into pagoda towers, watched soap bubbles glisten on the lips of wine glasses. Afterwards, while the two women dozed in their wicker armchairs in the bee-filled sunshine, he crept upstairs into their bedroom and opened the wardrobe door.

Back in his own room, he laid out on his bed the clothes he had borrowed from Méry, and those he had filched from his wife and child. He composed a toilette. He arrayed himself in stays, drawers, chemise, petticoat, stockings, and cherry silk dress; he pulled on the red wig Méry sometimes used for bedroom theatricals; he made up his face and forced his feet into high heels. He walked with small neat steps up and down his study, learning to manage his skirts and move his hips appropriately, learning a new gait, a new rhythm. Finally he checked his appearance one last time in the mirror over the fireplace, approaching his reflection and then retreating from it, flirting, curtsying and gracefully extending his hand gloved in lemon kid. Stephanie Mallarmé, poetess, had been born. He sat down at the table set in front of the window and began to write.

'A Throw of the Dice', Mallarmé's extraordinary experimental concrete poem, in which the text is flung and scattered and repeated in different type-sizes over successive pages, is universally recognized as his masterpiece, the patterns of dancing words evoking both chaos and a new order, the dawning of modernism, the creation of difficult beauty in the void left by God's exile. What is not so generally well known is the circumstance under which Mallarmé wrote it, dressed in women's clothes to facilitate the birth of a new kind of imagination, a radically different poetry. To put it simply: Stephanie could write things that Stephane could not.

Degas is supposed to have made several photographic portraits of Stephanie Mallarmé, but the plates have been lost. Some art historians think that Stephanie served as Degas' model for some of his studies of washerwomen and laundresses, but the matter remains in dispute.

NO HANDS

for Jim Latter

It began with the Virgin.

I picked her up in a bric-à-brac warehouse in Domfront in Normandy, *en route* to our little house in the Mayenne. She was standing behind the door unnoticed by everybody. Except for me. I saw her straight away. I got her at a knock-down price because she had no hands. Her arms ended in stumps. Apart from that disfigurement she was more or less intact. Her nose was chipped, and some of the paint on her oval face had flaked off. But her eyes and sash were still blue and the edging of the veil pleated around her forehead was still gold, and the roses under her bare feet were still faintly pink. Her expression was calm and distant.

As soon as I spotted her I wanted to give her a home. So we paid for her and wrapped her up in a blanket and put her in the boot of the car. Once upon a time she had been Our Lady of

Lourdes, the classic icon seen in every Catholic church throughout the land. But now she'd been thrown out, discarded as scrap, sold off cheap, she had lost her plaster sanctity and acquired a different mystery. I think it was to do with her missing hands.

A fairy story I read as a child, that I only dimly remember now, concerns the daughter of a miller who becomes known as the maiden with no hands. In the end she gets silver ones. It's all to do with riddles, a test of love between father and daughter. Can you love if you have no hands? The girl learns to survive through art, her own and the silversmith's. She survives the damage that's been inflicted on her by her father. Another way of telling the story is to say that she and her father loved each other too much. Their attachment could only end violently.

The hands of my plaster Virgin probably got knocked off by accident. They would have been laid together, slightly raised, in prayer. We had a similar statue at my convent school. In May we carried her in procession all round the nuns' garden, singing hymns as we walked. Our Lady of Lourdes was my mother to whom I prayed, begging her to forgive my sins. She was the refuge of sinners.

She originally appeared to Bernadette, a peasant girl born in the Pyrenees to a family so poor they lived in the disused local prison, a wretched place from which Bernadette escaped to watch over her uncle's sheep on the mountainside. She was not happy at home. She was often cold, hungry and ill. One day, collecting firewood by the river, she saw a beautiful girl perched high up on a shelf of the steep cliff, who spoke to her with great courtesy and tenderness and instructed her to reveal the spring of water hidden lower down in the rock. Bernadette obediently scrabbled in the dirt, and water gushed forth.

A country goddess; a kind and powerful mother; the *source* of water with magical and healing properties; they make a good story. I don't care that the Church got hold of it and twisted it into something pious and sentimental and saccharine. Bernadette was an artist. She created her own vision before it was taken away from her and travestied. She survived, like the miller's daughter in the fairy tale, by cherishing what was not there, what she'd lost. By filling up a gap with meaning.

So I liked my battered plaster Virgin with her missing hands, her invisible palms of air lightly touching, holding air between them. I decided not to replace those vanished fingers, nor to hide their absence with a bunch of flowers, but to display her as she was.

I tried her out in various places in the house. She was over two feet high, much taller than the statues my neighbours kept tucked away in alcoves beside their fireplaces or set in niches above their front doors. She didn't quite fit. She toppled and overbalanced between the jugs and saucepans in the kitchen. She got in the way on the sitting-room windowsill. She was too big for the mantelpiece. I didn't want my neighbours to think, when they dropped by for an aperitif, and saw her, nonchalantly raising her chopped wrists, that I was mocking their beliefs, their sturdy but discreet Catholicism. They were *croyants* though not *pratiquants*, believers who rarely attended Sunday Mass. The whole village turned out for a funeral, and for weddings and baptisms. But most people did not go to church otherwise and did not discuss God. *Le bon Dieu* was there and that was that.

The presence of *something else* could be witnessed all over the surrounding countryside. Him Up There, the one beloved of the *curé*, ruled the skies, but down here in the mud there were other gods, spirits of the wayside, their places marked with ancient boulders of granite carved into rough crosses. These had once been the signs of crossroads. At every lane branching off to a farm tucked away in the tiny valleys of the district, there was erected a stone cross, often decorated with a pattern, blurred by time and seasons, that might once have been a figure or a face. Then the Church came along and declared that these pagan symbols of crossroads, guarded by spirits, were in fact Christian crucifixes which only lacked, by some inexplicable omission, the nailed and bleeding figure of Christ. What Tim and I noticed, when we first came to live in the Mayenne, was how the goddess of the countryside reasserted herself in the face of these pious Catholic emblems. The granite boulders and stone crosses had niches carved in the middle of them, and into these little caves were set small statues of the Virgin. Inside the cross, at its heart, she had a place. So it was quite normal that Tim should come up with the idea of putting our plaster Virgin somewhere outside.

It took us over a year to hack down the wilderness of brambles and nettles at the side of the house. As we advanced into the tall thicket of thorns, as fierce and stout a barrier as the wall of roses around the Sleeping Beauty, we discovered a self-seeded plantation of elder and broom, ash and wild cherry, under the strangling embrace of the rampant blackberries. We ended up with a woodland garden interlaced with looping paths, thick with wild bushes and flowers which our puzzled neighbours called weeds and told us to spray with poison. At the far end of this narrow copse, which ran along the side of the hill against which the house was built, we put a bench, and just beyond this, on the brow of the gentle slope, we placed the Virgin, lodging her between boulders so that she stayed steady on her feet. This became a favourite place to sit and watch the sunset over the blue hills layering the horizon. Cows wandered in the green meadows just below, grazing, or lay under the apple trees. We would watch the distant roofs of our neighbour's barns turn glowing pink, drink a glass of wine, and chat about the day. The little Virgin stood like a sentinel to mark the boundary. Beyond her our land narrowed abruptly and fell down to a triangle of bramble and scrub, a loose, shifting pile of leaf-mould bristling with thorns that we hadn't bothered to clear. You couldn't see it from the bench. It was a reminder of what the whole garden had once been, a derelict wasteland full of rubbish.

One of the things I loved about the garden was the way it kept giving us gifts. There were all the trees it turned out to contain, and the wild flowers – drifts of mallow and poppies, cowslips and forget-me-nots and anemones and herb robert – and the holly and hawthorn hedges which were full of birds' nests, and the wild honeysuckle in the hedgerow which we coaxed to grow overhead along the arch of hazel overhanging our bench. Some of what the garden threw up was old debris: yards of broken barbed wire, rotten fence posts, old rabbit hutches and pigsties lying collapsed in the grass, and all the discarded bits and pieces of a household that hadn't had dustbins: mussel shells, whelk shells, mutton bones, empty perfume bottles, lengths of plastic string, scraps of old plastic sacks. The fragments of china that forced themselves out of the earth fascinated us. We picked them up and arranged them on the windowsills. Stencilled art-deco patterns in blue, wreaths of pink roses, flecks of yellow. Each distinct little bit suggested the whole it had once been part of. Sometimes we found several fragments of the same plate and tried to fit them together. Once, when we were rootling under the eaves removing the remains of an old wasps' nest, a pair of canvas baby's boots fell out, half rotted by age. So outside this house where so much was broken (ceilings and windows and doors) and needed to be restored, and in this garden where so much damaged stuff had been thrown away, the Virgin with her missing hands fitted perfectly.

People's lives had got broken too. The reason our house had originally been put up for sale at all, we discovered a year after we moved in, was because its owner had raped two of his five teenage daughters. Found out, cold-shouldered by the neighbours, he'd avoided a prison sentence because of his weak heart. He and his wife had sold us the house then got out.

Other stories emerged as more neighbours came round to visit and divulged to us, in fits and starts, as the whim took them, the history of the place. They told us who had been born in our sitting-room seventy years before, and about the American spy who had hidden in our garden in a dugout, and about how many local people had been shot by the Germans.

We fitted the stories together as best we could. Sometimes we couldn't understand all the words our new friends used, the dialect terms, and had to supply for ourselves what was missing. One of the stories was about the ruined mill-house across the lane at the far end of our garden, just beyond the triangle of brambles where the little Virgin kept watch.

We'd come across the miller's house by accident one afternoon, returning home from a walk. We were so entranced by the sound of splashing water behind the screen of trees and nettles on the steep bank that we fought our way into the tangled thicket. Behind it we found the millstream, fed by a waterfall tumbling between black rocks. Just alongside was the ruined house, roofless, half overgrown with ferns. Green moss furred its stone walls, green boughs swayed overhead, water flowed across the floor of bright green weeds. You could climb through the arched window down into the stream, then pick your way up the waterfall's steep staircase. It was a secret place. You couldn't tell, from the lane, that it was there. The woods had closed round it and swallowed it up. After our discovery, we would sit on our bench on summer nights and strain our ears to catch the splashing of the invisible waterfall on the other side of the lane and wish and wish that we had our own source of water on our land.

The mill-house had been lived in by the miller and his wife and their eleven children. After his wife died, the miller fell in love with his eldest daughter, who now kept house for him and the ten other children. When the girl came to her father and told him that she was leaving in order to marry her sweetheart, a young man from the village, the father went mad with jealousy and grief. One night, blind drunk, he set fire to the house and burned it down. All the children escaped and ran to their grandmother's. The father was put in prison and died in solitary confinement.

Most people get damaged at some time or other I think. More or less badly, with more or less chance of healing. So we grow into our own shapes, in the way that feet form the shapes of shoes and you can't step into those of someone else because they will never fit. I wonder who the baby was whose outgrown little canvas boots were thrown out casually into the garden? Perhaps they belonged to Monsieur Antoine Legré, who was born in the corner of our sitting-room seventy years ago. It was he who told us the story of the ruined house, sitting drinking Pernod in our kitchen, his small cheeks hard and red as cider apples.

My own damage had been on the inside and didn't show. A secret. Only I knew it was there. I was convinced it would never go away. Something inside me that had gone wrong and could not be put right. Something missing. I didn't know what it was. Only that I was afraid. Something terrible might happen. I didn't know what it was. When I fell in love with Tim and married him, my memory came back. I was able to remember the thirteen-year-old girl I'd been, in love with my dad and convinced I was the greatest sinner who walked this earth. I'd wanted to step into my mother's shoes and deserved eternal punishment. I didn't know how afraid I was that my father loved me too much. That something terrible might happen. I thought I was rubbish and should be cast out and left to rot. I deserved to be homeless; not to have a house. I was the maiden in the fairy story cutting off my hands, which longed for the wrong caresses, for a husband who wasn't mine. It took me thirty years to work out the answer to the riddle. I discovered what had been lacking when we bought the little house in France, the first property I'd ever owned, and Monsieur Legré told us his sad stories of the people who'd lived in it after him, and of the people who'd lived in the mill-house by the stream.

I let go of my guilt because I'd outgrown it. I dropped it like an old shoe. I let it rot down in the grass.

Tim and I cleared the last strip of the garden beyond the bench and the statue of the Virgin. She turned out to be indeed the goddess of the *source*, for after hacking our way through the brambles and extending the path over the brow of the slope down to the ivy-covered mound that had been concealed by branches of thorns, we found the sunken well that the people of the house had used in the old days, before the last owners had let it fall into disuse. It had always been there, waiting to be rediscovered. Its mouth was clogged with earth. Our next task, as we knew from the fairy tales, was to dig down into the dirt for the water, and release the secret spring hidden in the hillside, so that even in the scorching heat of summer the garden could be kept fertile and green.

LES MENUS PLAISIRS

for Julian Barnes

My older sister was the pretty one whereas I was plain. When there are two of you, people do make comparisons. You learn how much beauty matters to them, or its lack. My sister had thick shiny brown hair, hazel eyes with long lashes, and fine skin. She was good, too, though in bitchy moments I thought of her as merely innocent, and she was clever as well. She was going to university in the autumn, to read chemistry. I was a year younger, studying for my A levels in art history and English and French literature. Useless subjects, as my father pointed out, when it came to getting a job. I might have a face like a scone but I was handy at home. I could cook. Mum worked all kinds of odd hours at the hospital; often she was on nights; and so I took charge in the kitchen.

Our father liked his food, but it had to be British. Suet pudding was one of his favourites, a yellow hill studded with raisins wrinkled as rocks, the sides sliced then slabbed with cold butter on to which sugar fell crunchy as snow. More sugar sifted on to the morning porridge, the crust of the apple pie, the Eccles cakes, the Bakewell tart. Food was treated like gentlemen callers in a Victorian novel: it was interrogated as to its intentions, its culture and origins. Paella, spaghetti and couscous were forbidden suitors at our door. No daughter of mine, our father seemed to imply, will keep company with a sweet potato, a mango, a yam.

Kippers he enjoyed, bitter marmalade, Cheddar cheese, toad-in-the-hole, the occasional Brussels sprout, a well-risen Yorkshire to accompany the Sunday roast. Luckily for us, lovers of spices, curry was also deemed thoroughly British, which is to say decent and honourable and partaken of on Saturday nights after the pub; it sneaked in past the suspicious bouncer at the larder door.

Nursery food pleased Dad the best, comfort food for wintry weather: lemon sponge with custard, bangers and mash, bacon sandwiches, oxtail soup. Once, on a rainy May evening, dreaming of summer in hot climates such as I'd read about in novels, I served up a ratatouille. Dad had not previously been introduced to ratatouille. He eyed the minced parsley I'd sprinkled over the thick tomato sauce, the sheen of oil on the onion chunks I'd carefully forked to the top of the dish. He demanded to know the names of the other ingredients. On being informed that these included red peppers, courgettes, aubergines, garlic and olive oil, he snarled, None of your filthy foreign muck in my house, seized the dish and flung it into the back garden.

I became a vegetarian. What other form of rebellion was open to me? Sex was out of the question, since I was so plain; drugs were not as easily available then as they are now; and drink didn't interest me because the alcohol at home, sherry and port kept in the sideboard for Christmas, tasted too thick and sweet. Dad went out for his nightly pint; the rest of us drank orange squash. I'd never had wine. And I lacked the courage to visit the off-licence on my own. But at least I could choose what to eat. Cheese on toast mainly, the frozen-pea part of Sunday lunch, apples, bananas and pears. I made salads that no one else wanted: wet leaves of crisp Cos lettuce like long boats, cold baked beans, quarters of tomato and slices of beetroot, salad cream. On our rare Sunday picnics, I served the others pork pies and ham rolls and packed soggy tomato sandwiches for myself.

My sister rebelled too. She went off to Paris for the summer, to work as an au pair. Dad tried to forbid it, but Mum stuck up for her. The poor girl needs a break, she insisted: all work and no play. My sister whirled off on the boat train, triumphantly clutching her brown leather suitcase, wearing her new green mohair skirt and blue winklepickers.

She promised to write to me, and she did. She was obviously lonely at first, a bit homesick, despite all the glamour of Paris. The family was quite posh, apparently, but very nice. The mother was about forty, very thin, and fashionably dressed, and the father roughly the same age, very good-looking. The two little girls were nice. The son was nice. Plane trees, the metro, a trip to the Louvre, were all nice too.

My sister's language only livened up when it came to food. She listed what she ate, because she knew it would interest me; perhaps she wanted to tantalize me too. Fat pink and white asparagus with hollandaise, new broad beans in cream sauce, tarragon eggs in aspic, artichokes, spinach soufflé, carrots simmered in butter and white wine. My sister reported that she had put on a bit of weight. The father said it suited her. The son said so too. He was called Aimé after his father, he was very handsome like him and very nice.

That was in June. In July my sister continued her reports on gourmandise, the peaches and nectarines sliced into red wine, the redcurrants and raspberries heaped around sugar-sprinkled cream cheese, but her letters altered in character. They became the equivalent, in writing, of whispers and giggles. Of boasts.

She had fallen in love. I had to swear not to tell. The affair had to remain a secret so that Madame did not find out and send her packing. Sex, she scrawled, was fantastic. She slept in the former maid's room, which was on the floor above the main flat, over the kitchen, connected to it by a back staircase of coiling iron, so that she was at some distance from the family. This was most convenient for lovers' trysts. Her beloved crept into her room in the middle of the night, when everyone else was asleep, and they made love in the dark, so that not a crack of light would show under the door to anyone peering up from the bottom of the spiralling stair. It was much more exciting when you couldn't see the other person's face. More mysterious. More sexy.

I wrote back: But who is it? What's his name? And my sister replied: It's Aimé, of course. I told you. I told you his name before.

But which one? I didn't dare ask.

Two weeks passed. My sister did not write again. My parents did not worry. They shrugged and said: She's young, she's enjoying herself, no news is good news. They were horrified when I suggested telephoning Paris. Long-distance calls abroad, via the operator, were something you only made on Christmas Day, when sending duty greetings to relatives just before the Queen's Speech. My parents were planning a week away themselves, to a rented caravan in the Isle of Wight. That was as far south as my father was prepared to go. He was looking forward to fish and chips, cockles and whelks from the stall outside the pub, crab and salmon sandwiches for high tea. I forbore to point out that the fish might have swum in from somewhere foreign like France, or somewhere even more exotic. I kept my mouth shut for once.

I was to stay at home and feed the cat. I made my parents a picnic lunch they could eat by the roadside – Cornish pasties, hard-boiled eggs and fruit cake – and waved them off as they sped away in the Hillman Imp.

Then I added together the contents of my piggybank and the charity box in the front hall, swept up the cash my mother had left me for housekeeping and emergencies, dropped the keys of our house in to the next-door neighbour and set off for Paris to rescue my sister. I wore my box-pleated brown skirt that I had got in the C&A sale for twelve and sixpence, my yellow blouse, and my brown school shoes. I didn't take a suitcase because I didn't think I'd be staying in Paris that long. I took my tartan handbag, packed with a spare pair of knickers and a toothbrush.

My first meal in Paris was breakfast at a pavement café just outside the Gare du Nord: coffee, a piece of baguette spread with butter, and a croissant. My French accent didn't seem too bad; the waiter understood me without any difficulty. I felt filled with courage, as a result. Just as well when I considered the tasks that lay ahead. Everything seemed much less clear-cut since I'd got off the boat train.

Making love was completely normal in France, whether with glamorous older men or virile young ones. I had learned that from the novels I had to read for A level French literature. My sister's behaviour was not therefore odd at all. The street in which I sat dawdling over my coffee was thronged with people hurrying to work in the sunshine. Every one of them might have a lover or a mistress, for all I knew. It didn't seem to have done them any harm. How well-dressed and confident everybody looked. Not a box-pleated skirt in sight. Not a single boat-shaped brown school shoe. It now occurred to me, as I wetted my finger and picked up every last buttery flake of my croissant, that my sister might not want to be rescued at all. Perhaps I was simply being jealous and envious and trying to spoil her fun. Perhaps I was just a puritan and a prig.

Probably I shouldn't have come to Paris at all.

Having got this far on my quest, however, I would have to go through with it to the bitter end. At the very least I could go and visit my sister. I could drop by. I could pretend I was just passing and thought I'd look in on her. I could say I brought a message from our parents, that they hoped she wasn't finding French food too greasy and rich, not too much olive oil and everything swimming in butter.

I plunged into the metro. I liked the way the doors of the carriages slid together and met with a hiss of rubber lips, a pneumatic kiss, then sprang apart again when you wielded the lever to open them. I liked the poetry of the station names, a mapped web of strange words that made me feel oddly safe, that the work of connection had been done for me and I could not get lost. Then the indigo letters of my stop glided past the door and I jumped out of the train.

I trailed through echoing tunnels, pushed through the narrow exit gates, trod up the steep stone staircase under the art-nouveau arch of looped iron lace, erupted into another Paris. The metro had suspended time; I'd had no sensation of travelling; I'd been in a subterranean world of foreign languages ordered in new ways. Now, re-emerging into the daylight, the sunshine, I felt as though I'd been magically transported, snatched up by high winds, carried by them, as though they were great hands, across the city, and dumped down here in this quiet side-street lined with plane trees shading balconied buildings.

The house-numbers were set high on the wall, blue and white enamel signs. Number five was in the middle of a long stone façade. The doorbells were on one side of an archway. The small door cut in the big one was open. I went through, past what I guessed must be the concierge's lodge, and up the staircase opposite. I swivelled up to the fourth floor, found the brass plate, set into heavy mahogany, with the family's name on it, pressed the buzzer nearby. The door swung open and I stumbled forwards into the dark.

– Don't try and look, he said: don't even dare try and look.

I couldn't see anything. Blackness pressed my eyes shut, a soft cloth. I waited for the command which meant we could begin.

– Open your mouth.

His voice was a whisper. Coaxing, teasing. His finger tapped my cheek. Once, twice.

The cold tip of what must be a spoon prodded my lips, pushed them gently apart. I felt the spoon tilt, deliver its heaped cargo. Something grainy and loose fell on to my tongue. All my senses were alert, clamouring, as though food, when invisible, not only tasted and smelled but also sang to you. *Allegro*. Whatever it was was lukewarm. We had agreed on that in advance. Nothing too hot. No scorching surprises.

I shifted my tongue, with its little savoury burden, from side to side. I chewed once then swallowed.

I was sitting on a chrome and leather chair, and to help myself concentrate I gripped the smooth sides of the seat with my hands, then wriggled my fingers under my woollen knees. I clenched all my muscles tight as I tried to decide, then unclenched them again.

I could feel him watching me. Cool air was blowing in through the open kitchen window behind me and caressing the back of my neck.. His warm breath was close to my face.

I licked my lips. Delicious, whatever it was. I was salivating for more.

– Lentils, I guessed: no, not big enough. *Flageolets verts*.

He laughed.

– No. White haricot beans.

The air changed in density as he leaned over me to untie the blindfold. His fingers brushed my ears as he struggled to untie the knot. The tea-towel fell into my lap and Aimé's blue eyes shone at me. He pulled at my sleeve.

– Now let's change places. Now it's my turn.

Aimé was eight years old and always on the lookout for new games to play indoors when it was raining and we could not go out. I had remembered the food game from my brief experience as a Brownie long ago. In Paris I discovered that mushrooms fried in butter, if you bit into them blindfolded, tasted remarkably like steak. That if you ate two leaves of salad separately, at a certain interval, you wouldn't necessarily know they were both lettuce.

I also discovered my sister Psyche's powers of imagination. Aimé senior was a small, balding civil servant who dozed off in his armchair after supper most nights, exactly like Dad. His plump wife was as kind as could be, inviting me to stay with the family for my week's holiday and only too pleased that I enjoyed helping Psyche take care of the three small children. I shared the maid's room with my sister, at the top of the little back staircase, which had kept the maid unseen by the family, a pair of invisible serving hands. Psyche would sit on the kitchen floor with the two little girls, playing with the dolls' house, which was a cardboard miniature of the palace at Versailles, while Aimé and I sat at the table, working our way through all the combinations of tastes we could dream up. A couple of times he tricked me into eating meat and fish. A mouthful of cold jellied veal. A sliver of baked trout. I didn't mind. To him I was a barbarian, a fanatic alien, with my insistence on sticking to eating things that didn't have feet. I enjoyed his attempts at taming me, trying to change my odd ways.

The family had never heard of vegetarianism and so they considered it bizarre. It wasn't in their culture, that was all. They were surprised when I pointed out how many non-meat dishes they ate as a matter of course. Leek and potato soup. Onion tart. Stuffed pancakes *au gratin*. Stuffed tomatoes. Rice salad. Haricots *à la crème*. *Pommes Anna*. *Pommes dauphinoises*. Courgette soufflé. Cheese fritters. And the food from Vietnam and Algeria and Tunisia which was sold all round the city. We ate spring rolls and beansprouts and couscous and *brik à l'oeuf* as a matter of course. They were considered French dishes.

I thought that what French people needed was a good vegetarian cookery book full of classic French recipes. Vegetarianism would be bound to catch on eventually. After I'd finished my A levels and had trained as a chef I might open a vegetarian restaurant in Paris. Aimé wanted to come in as my partner. We decided to call the restaurant Bliss.

I got home the day before Mum and Dad were due back from their holiday. The cat returned from next door, sleek and fat. Over the rest of the summer I played a new version of the food game with Dad. I cooked him French dishes but gave them English names. *Filet de boeuf en croûte* became beef Wellington. *Crème patissière* was custard. Et cetera. He swallowed my deception. It slipped down a treat.

THE SHEETS

— I've got someone rather special arriving next week, Mrs Bertie breathed down the telephone: get out the best sheets for him, will you? Those linen ones with the monogram that I bought last week at the *brocante* fair.

Sooner or later I'd find out what was up . . . She was not discreet, Mrs Bertie. She dyed her hair yellow, painted her lips scarlet and her toenails silver, and wore cotton-lycra T-shirts and short skirts that hugged her lean figure. Her husband might have run off with a younger woman but she was gallantly insisting that life began again at fifty. She refused to act her age and didn't worry about mutton dressed as lamb. You're only as old as you feel, she asserted. I enjoyed her clichés. They seemed true. They were a shorthand I understood.

I did the beds for her. I went in on the Saturday morning, as soon as the visitors had departed, put the used sheets in the washing-machine, and got out the clean ones for the people arriving later that afternoon. I swept and dusted, wiped round the bathroom and kitchen, bagged up the rubbish. Then I laid kindling and logs ready for a fire, put a welcoming bottle of white wine in the fridge and a bunch of flowers on the table. That was the sort of little personal touch that pleased the guests.

Mrs Bertie, cosseting her customers, did good business. Some of them came back every year. There was nothing much for these tourists to do except go for walks, sit in the garden, and visit old churches. There was no swimming-pool, which meant that people with children didn't rent the house. No sticky-fingered toddlers smeared chocolate on the embroidered tablecloths. No teenagers with ghetto-blasters drowned out the hoarse song of crickets, the distant chiming of church bells. That was precisely Mrs Bertie's selling-point. She catered for what she called discerning tastes and charged accordingly. She provided not only comfort and a maid service, but also a particular ambience, decorating her old stone farmhouse in the town-dweller's version of peasant style. Straw-seated wooden armchairs were drawn up around the vast fireplace. Kelims strewed the red-tiled floors. Oak chests displayed collections of Quimper bowls and jugs. *Faux-naïf* oils of cockerels and pigs, done by Mr Bertie before he scarpered, hung in the lime-washed sitting-room. Ancient cookery utensils and hanging bunches of herbs decorated the kitchen, where all the modern equipment was hidden inside painted cupboards distressed to look antique. Drifts of white lace screened the bedroom windows.

Her guests pronounced her décor charming and original and utterly authentic and exclaimed how much at home it made them feel. For my taste there were too many quaint little still-life arrangements of pebbles, old wooden cotton-reels and bread-baskets lying about, too many clusters of fat beeswax candles, too many casual throws of Provençal fabric draping the armchairs, but my opinion didn't matter. Mrs Bertie didn't pay me to criticize her artless displays of earthenware *rillettes* pots and pierced cream-cheese moulds. These were set out not for my delectation but as lures. She sold them, with a fine show of reluctance, to those clients renting the house who begged especially hard for a souvenir. No, Mrs Bertie paid me to look after the place and be around for the guests while she got on with her main business. This was buying junk and ferrying it back across the Channel to sell as antiques. It was astonishing, she told me once, watching sharp-eyed as I hoovered, the prices that old blue enamelware, mottled and speckled, could fetch down the Portobello Road. Milk churns, lidded salt boxes, racks for ladles and slotted spoons: people couldn't get enough of them. The items that would never sell to the discerning bourgeoisie in France – for example douching-pots complete with spouts and rubber hose – she picked up for noth-ing at farm sales, took to London and foisted off, *sans* rubber bits, as unusually shaped vases, to unsuspecting foreigners.

I was currently the maid service she advertised in her brochure. Unemployment being what it was round here, I was glad of the job. Tired of secondary-school teaching, newly single after the break-up of a long-term affair, I had moved to France three years previously, when I had bought the village café. The owners had just died, and their children, wanting to be rid of it, had put it up for sale. The café had wooden shutters patched with flaking pale green paint, an iron door that scraped, and a blue slate roof. It faced the public urinal and the church on the tiny *place*, had a *boulangerie* on one side and an *épicerie* on the other. Inside, the décor was all brown lino, brown and orange wallpaper, orange Formica, and brown and orange sunburst tiles. Outside, the café sported three rusty metal tables in the shade of a cracked awning. I felt it was waiting for me to rescue it. I fell in love instantly. Sentimental or what? Anyway, I blew all my savings on it.

I decided to go for touches of the early seventies retro look. I painted the walls with a *trompe l'oeil* of psychedelic wallpaper in purple and cream, pulled up the lino to reveal the old green and white floor tiles underneath, installed a juke-box and a football game, both salvaged from the local scrap merchant, polished the zinc counter, hung up my posters of Simone Signoret, Brigitte Bardot and Jeanne Moreau, and stocked the glass shelves with bottles of pastis, Dubonnet and Orangina arranged on circles of paper lace.

I expected to run a flourishing outfit. I thought I might expand, might even achieve Routier status and provide fifty-five-franc set-menu lunches for passing drivers. But I failed to hold on to the old clientele let alone attract an additional one. Shortly after I moved in, a supermarket opened in our nearest town, and my neighbours, the bakery and grocery, both closed. Then the parish priest, aged eighty, finally retired. There was a shortage of priests, and the new *curé*, when he was eventually appointed, had to look after five villages. The church was now shut three Sundays out of four, and so with no big Sunday rush, when people poured out of Mass ready for a chat with friends and neighbours over an aperitif, the café ran down. I had to admit defeat and cease trading.

I liked the village well enough and decided to stay on, for the time being at least. So I continued living in the café. I left the faded sign in 1950s lettering above the door intact. I began to earn a frugal income acting as caretaker for the local *maisons secondaires*. These were used for just a couple of months each year, when people arrived on holiday from Paris or from England. The owners could rest easy the remainder of the time, knowing that I kept an eye on their precious properties. I dropped in to each *fermette* once a week to ensure that everything was generally ticking over all right, checked the fuse boxes and water pipes, mowed and weeded in season, cleaned when asked to do so. I grew my own vegetables, did not require new clothes, and ran an ancient Citroën. I got by. In the evenings I listened to music and read.

Mrs Bertie let out her *gîte* almost all year round. She herself didn't want to live in it, in the depths of the countryside, four kilometres from the village, preferring the tiny house she had bought for herself just along the street from mine. Sometimes we dropped in to see each other in the evenings, if she wasn't away driving her van of dubious antiques over to England, but we maintained a certain reserve, leaving plenty of space for withdrawal, should this ever become necessary. I think she was lonely sometimes, as lonely as I was, but we neither of us admitted it. Our friendship was limited to the kind of things you could say over a glass of Ricard. We discussed cookery and gardening and fiction. I stuck to contemporary French writers, in order to brush up my vocabulary. My employer constantly struggled to decide on her favourite English novelist. She felt you should only have one, which meant she read very widely and also regularly changed her mind. At the moment she admired the works of Peter Lofthouse. She said he wrote brilliantly about women.

I went over to Mrs Bertie's *gîte* as usual, late on the Saturday morning, and was surprised to find her Renault van parked at the gate. Normally she left me to my tidying-up and did not interfere. Today she was wearing knee-length khaki shorts, tightly belted at the waist, a pink vest, pink and silver earrings, and a pair of silver mules with kitten heels. Her hair was newly blonded. Her bare arms and legs were already golden brown, rather too obviously aided by a bottle of fake tan. Her toenails were coral, to match her lips.

She had clearly been giving the house and garden, as well as herself, a rapid makeover. A white voile curtain fluttered at the front door, which stood wide and welcoming. Fresh muslin framed the open kitchen window. The gravelled yard in front of the house, normally a clear space where people parked their cars and had barbecues, was now set with groups of blue-painted tubs. Four lavender bushes, and four little bay trees, clipped into pom-poms, flanked a couple of rose bushes thick with red blooms. Two hibiscus, laden with pale pink blossoms, flared at each end of this arrangement. Large terracotta pots of salmon pink geraniums lined the steps up to the front door.

Mrs Bertie had always held out against the massed summer displays of scarlet, crimson and pink geraniums and petunias so beloved of all our village neighbours. From June onwards every year the white fronts of their houses dripped with gaudy colour.

Balconies and window-boxes shrieked with fuchsia and magenta. Ivy geraniums flopped, fleshy and red, out of every window, like hot tongues lolling on lips. Mrs Bertie, so unrestrained in matters of personal adornment, held herself back when it came to gardening. She believed that annuals should be sown in hazy drifts of blue, mauve and white, with the merest sprinkling of pink, just an occasional dot of yellow or red for contrast's sake, against an overwhelmingly green background of feathery grass, shrubs and trees. She deprecated the tightly packed whorls of technicolour bedding plants that emblazoned the local roundabouts and signalled the whereabouts of *mairies* and railway stations. She declared the French taste for unrelieved brilliance vulgar and flashy. Now, I saw, she had suddenly succumbed to it. She had relented, and allowed a blushing tide to wash over her house. As though she'd rouged it. The buds on her geraniums gleamed like the tips of lipsticks.

She was squatting on her heels potting the last of these flowers when I arrived, a plastic sack of compost, torn open at the top, beside her, a stack of empty plant trays toppling nearby. Her fingertips pressed quickly, tenderly, into the black mould, fitting the plant neatly in, tucking the earth down around it, patting the surface flat, caressing the red-brown rim as she spun the pot to view the effect from every angle.

She smiled at me and waggled her fingers at her handiwork.

– He's a novelist, she said, as though that explained everything: he's taken the house for six weeks, to work on his new novel.

Her tone was reverent and excited. As though she'd been awarded a medal for long service or been made a Dame.

– His name? I asked.

She clasped a geranium in front of her with both hands like a bouquet and bent her face reverently over it. I can remember seeing big beefy men at Columbia Road flower market in east London look like that, making their way back through the crowds with their purchases off the stalls, their arms encircling enormous bunches of dahlias and gladioli, protectively holding the paper cones of delphiniums and stocks and sweet williams out in front of them lest they be crushed, faces as rapt and serious as brides'. Mrs Bertie had that same incongruous charm, I suppose because she was tough and skinny as a boy, despite all her furbelows, often to me she looked like a boy in drag, and none the worse for that, and now her brown brittleness had suddenly gone all caramel-melted, all creamy-soft.

She paused. I knew what name she would pronounce. I watched her face break open into unashamed delight.

Her voice cracked a little when she spoke. She was trying to sound normal and brisk.

– It's Peter Lofthouse. Can you imagine? He found us through the Internet, apparently. He's due in an hour's time, so we'd better get a move on.

My attention was distracted by a bee circling the pink and lavender frills of the sweetpeas she'd set in a jug on the kitchen windowsill. The pastel ruffles were just like the dancers' costumes in a Degas painting, framed by the muslin curtains as though they indeed belonged to sturdy girls stretching their legs and arms into strange postures on a stage. Degas liked to paint the play of muscle. His women demonstrate their strong, flexible backs, the possible curve, almost to painfulness, of shoulders and knees. His ballerinas, like his nudes, are not at all delicate; they are as concentrated and purposeful as flowers. It occurred to me that Degas might have liked to paint Mrs Bertie. I thought that with her clothes off she wouldn't look half bad.

She rose to her feet and reached for the watering-can. The bee made up its mind and dived into the skirts of a sweetpea. You could practically hear it slurping.

– I'll get on with the beds, then, I said.

– Bed, she said: just the one. He's coming on his own.

I got out the linen sheets, smooth from eighty years of use, with a raised silky monogram ornamenting the top edge decorated in drawn-threadwork, and made up the double bed in the main bedroom. I whisked round and did my usual cleaning while she cleared up outside. We both left in good time. Mrs Bertie made a point of never being present when guests arrived. She believed that it was intrusive and over-controlling, spoiled their pleasure at discovering the house for themselves. She left handwritten notes on the kitchen table instead, explaining how everything worked, and a list of useful telephone numbers, including mine as caretaker.

At home, I sat in my tiny back garden, which was mainly vegetable plot, and ate my lunch. Bread and butter and *saucisson*, a few gherkins, a pear, a glass of ice-cold cider. I thought how manfully Mrs Bertie had resisted the temptation to hang around and meet her famous guest, despite admiring him so much, how bravely she had obeyed her own protocol and tactfully removed herself from the *gîte* before he drove up. He wouldn't know, but I did, what the tubs and pots of flowers meant. I thought that perhaps Mrs Bertie herself didn't know either. She probably just called it trying to make the place look nice. Ship-shape and Bristol-fashion. Would he notice the PL monogram on the sheets? She must have bought them as an act of half-unconscious veneration and *aide-mémoire*, it was the kind of obsessive, secret homage people in love pay to their absent idols, but without ever daring to imagine he would one day lie between them. I wondered if Mrs Bertie had read Stendhal on love, on how it saturates everything in your world, a dipped rod clustering with crystals. I wondered if Peter Lofthouse had.

Two days later I was digging up nettles from a neglected corner of my garden when someone banged and rattled on the street door. I tore off my work gloves, mopped my sweaty face, and went through.

– Are you open? he asked: can I get a beer? I walked in from the place I'm staying at and I'm very thirsty.

Peter Lofthouse had turquoise eyes. He was a tall, sturdy man in his mid-fifties, with brown crewcut hair. He was wearing a pair of old jeans, and a T-shirt of faded indigo, very clean, patched with sweat. I looked back at him and my insides leaped about.

I decided that I could expand maid service to bar service. I waved him in and found him a cold beer. We sat out the back in deck-chairs and I explained about buying the café and working for Mrs Bertie. That was the effect he had on me: I wanted to tell him things, make up stories for him, make him laugh.

He took to walking into the village most afternoons. He would get up early and write all morning, before the heat struck, then have lunch and a siesta, then go for a walk. In the evenings he went back to the *gîte* and revised the day's work. He seemed pleased to have found a friend. We didn't talk much about literature. When we weren't making love in my bedroom upstairs we played bar football or fooled about with the juke-box. Sometimes we went swimming in the local lake. Sometimes he asked me over for a barbecue.

Mrs Bertie rationed herself to one half-hour visit to the *gîte* per week, late on Saturday mornings, arriving while I was strolling around with a mop. Peter always stopped work and came out to greet her. He accepted her gift, whatever it was that week, a home-made mocha cake or some almond biscuits, with his devastating smile. He bent his head and listened courteously to her rush of dippy talk. The shyer she felt the more clichés she uttered, but he didn't appear to notice. He wrote kind dedications in all the copies of his novels she brought him to sign. She was pink under the force of his charm. Probably it was just good manners, she said to me later, but he made me feel I was the bee's knees. I agreed. He had that effect on me as well. Mrs Bertie pretended to be merely the attentive hostess but her eyes shone too much. She would tell him how proud she was that his new novel was taking shape in her house, and then she would blush even more, and dash away again.

After her departure he and I would have lunch together. I brought the food with me and cooked for him, and he provided the wine. It became our Saturday ritual. Funny how you can establish rituals in just six weeks. I had found some curly white iron chairs and a table in one of the sheds, had rubbed off the rust spots and slapped on a coat of paint. We would sit and eat at the side of the house, in the shade of the lilacs, away from the white glare of the gravel. I got out Mrs Bertie's best damask tablecloth and napkins, I dared to use her best crystal glasses, I built pyramids of peaches and nectarines crowned with wreaths of roses, I laid the cheeses on fans of walnut leaves, I raided the garden for thyme and nasturtium flowers to sprinkle on the salad. I was just like Mrs Bertie, wanting to give Peter gifts. He was as kind to me as he was to her, as I speculated he was to everybody. I supposed he was used to being fallen in love with. People falling at his feet, right and left, in droves.

At the end of the six weeks he departed. We said our goodbyes in my bedroom, lying in each other's arms in the sweaty heat, the afternoon before he went.

– Ring me next time you're in London, Simon, won't you? he said: we could meet for a drink.

I didn't know whether he lived with someone special. I hadn't asked him because I hadn't wanted to find out. I thought I'd never forget his smell. He smelt of hay and flowers and oranges and sweat.

Next morning, when I got to the *gîte*, he was already gone. Mrs Bertie's van was parked on the gravel. When I went upstairs to strip his bed I found her lying in it, between his sheets, face pressed into his pillow, one hand clutching the silky monogram that formed part of the decoration of the drawn-threadwork edge. Her clothes were on the floor.

– One last sniff, she said to me later, downstairs, over the last of the white wine: you make your bed and then you lie on it, don't you?

She began telling me about a new novelist she had discovered called Griff Jones. Peter had lent her one of his novels. She thought that he really might be the one this time. Apparently he wrote brilliantly about the interiors of houses.

– Plenty more fish in the sea, she said to me over her brimming glass: never say die.

FLUENCY

It is odd, now that I think about it, that I have never considered Paris as a possible home. Yet I'm sure it could have been perfectly feasible. As a photographer I could have worked anywhere. My French is not as fluent as I'd like, but I speak well enough to get by. My French always improves, anyway, when I'm actually in France, surrounded by French sounds; soaked in them; saturated. Perhaps I've simply hung on to holiday cliché, a wornout dream of romance, wanted to keep Paris as my special Somewhere Else, my paradise, the golden city in which I experience life as intensively and ecstatically as though I were on acid. This visionary bliss is not designed to survive daily reality. If I lived in Paris then I'd have to become a tourist to somewhere else instead. London, probably.

I've carefully kept Paris as my place of pilgrimage by associating it with the pursuit of particular beloved artist or writer ghosts, tracking down their flats and studios and favourite cafés, or with epiphanies of various sorts: those four small Vuillards I discovered in the Musée d'Orsay last year, for example, on that June day smelling of hot dust, lime blossom and vanilla, that day when I wandered into the little gallery in the rue de Seine and met Pierre for the first time. I've gone to Paris with all my lovers, for doomed or magical or awkward weekends. Each different lover provided a different view of the city, different museums and art galleries for us to frequent, dawdling hand in hand or arm in arm, different cafés and bars for us to lounge in while we talked. And because I haven't always had the courage of my convictions and desires, and so haven't had all that many lovers, I cannot claim to know Paris very well. I need a map, a bus guide, a plan of the metro, to get me around. A few metro stations shine for ever with my lovers' names superimposed on them, written up above the entrances to those labyrinthine underworlds in loops of stars.

I had assumed I was finished with Paris as a site of assignation. That I could return to it as just another destination and get to know it properly. No more secret passions. No more mad fantasies. I certainly never intended to fall in love again. All that was over and gone. The pain and suffering and loss – all finished. Now I would learn to love Paris as I loved London, with a modicum of calm. Now I'd visit Paris simply as a reasonable adult, as a professional photographer happily trawling the streets.

London is the city in which I grew up, got married and reared four children, the city in which I have become a widow and grown old. I know London and how its districts fit together as well as I know how to spell my own name. I don't depend in London on the company of other people to make discoveries. I go by myself.

And I never put a foot or a letter wrong. I have learned London so well simply by walking around it, combing and recombing its tangled patterns of streets, ever since I first left my parents' house over forty years ago.

When I was young I moved about a lot. I lived in bedsits, communal houses and squats in different districts: Pimlico, Finsbury Park, Holloway, Clapham Junction, Stepney, Stoke Newington, Notting Hill, Bayswater, Holland Park. For twenty years, with John, I lived in Bethnal Green. Now I am sixty and I live alone in a tiny flat in Stew Lane in the City, near St Paul's, within the sound of Bow Bells. Until last month I could see St Paul's out of my bedroom window, if I leaned out far enough, but now the derelict warehouses, on the other side of Stew Lane, are being renovated to become a block of luxury flats, and the surging concrete-pillared six-floor high-rise building cuts off my view. I don't mind. There's a better view from the communal roof terrace, anyway, across the river to the Globe and Bankside.

As a girl of eighteen up from the suburbs, exploring London at weekends, I prowled around the City on Sundays. I loved its emptiness, its grand buildings, and the names of its streets. In the suburb where I lived the roads and cul-de-sacs and crescents had faked-up names purporting to evoke a bucolic and pastoral idyll of the past, the vanished farmland of Middlesex that had been paved over to make way for these meek estates of mock-Tudor, names like Fairmead and Bullscroft which seemed to me wishy-washy and sentimental. Whereas the City names were signposts that pointed to images from poetry, the history of religion, a trading past that remained vibrantly real. Milk Street, Bread Street, Paternoster Lane, Godliman Lane, Saffron Hill, Garlick Hill. I recited the words to myself as though I strung beads on a rosary, I sang litanies of freedom. I discovered Sir Christopher Wren's house, opposite St Paul's on the far bank of the river, whence, I learned, he would emerge every morning to be rowed across the busy tide to superintend the building of his great work, and I climbed over the back wall to explore the garden. I wandered the deserted quays, scrambling past Keep Out signs and under fences of barbed wire, diving in and out of crumbling alleys. I remembered Lucy Snowe, in *Villette*, coming to London for the first time, arriving in darkness, lying in bed in her small and ancient hotel and suddenly realizing, as she hears the loud bells ring out, that she lies in the shadow of St Paul's.

A lot of those streets and alleys got bombed to smithereens in the war. A lot of other places got pulled down in the postwar rush to modernize, the love affair with concrete. Now the City has been restored, rebuilt, reinvented. It's an image, refurbished and repainted, of its former self. Now I myself live in the City, which I never dreamed, all those years ago, could ever be possible, bang opposite Sir Christopher Wren's house, which is still standing in the tiny terrace that squeezes in alongside the spanking-new pretend-old Globe, and I stand on the roof of my block of flats, leaning on the parapet, to stare across, and I remember that optimistic girl I was, with her flared loons and strings of beads and wild hair. Going wherever she fancied. Trespassing. Breaking and entering. Falling easily in love. Nowadays you can walk along the river all the way from Westminster through into Blackfriars, past our little block at Queenhythe, and eastwards past gleaming malls and through cobbled narrow streets as clean as film sets into shiny Wapping. At dusk the strings of silvery lights switch on, and the cafés serving cappuccino and smart fashionable food sparkle enticingly. All stage managed. A brilliant spectacle, a newness that is both dazzling and disturbing.

Loving to walk through London, by night or day, taught me to look at things. That was what made me a photographer: my fascination with the material of streets, with street furniture, with the fabric of which the city is made. Strolling eye to eye with windows whose cracked stone sills sprouted feathery weeds, with old brick walls streaked with subtle colours, blue and yellow on pink and brown, spotting the ghosts of old stencilled ads on the sides of Victorian shops, the decorative details of iron railings, the bits of debris caught by the sturdy grilles over kerbside drains where the water swirled black and shiny in the gutters, the design of fire hydrants and telephone boxes. People warned of rapists and muggers but I refused to fear my fellow-citizens. I strode aggressively when necessary, glaring and growling if I had to, clad in a huge old coat and big boots. I did not look vulnerable. I knew the street codes. Even as a naïve girl too wide-eyed for her own good, I escaped all harm.

Aged sixty, I still go for long walks around London, and of course continue to discover parts of it I haven't known before. Walking home from the West End along the Strand and Fleet Street, for example, I slip in and out of the yards and passages lacing together the riverside and the Law Courts and the gardens of the Temple and the secret pubs hidden at the back of slits between shops, and I think of Virginia Woolf walking there and thinking of Defoe and Dr Johnson doing exactly the same thing. Or I explore north through the back-streets of Smithfield, Clerkenwell, Finsbury, Angel. A magical incantation, every time, sings in my head, of names and places. Blake went for long walks like these, weaving north and south, Hampstead to Westminster to Peckham Rye. Keats, while he studied at Guy's, had lodgings in Borough, just a stone's throw away from me. Mrs Gaskell thought nothing of walking up to Highgate and back in a single afternoon.

I like wandering aimlessly, with no fixed goal, unsure exactly where I will end up, letting my feet choose their own route, as the whim takes them. Mapping the City I once knew on to the City that I live in now, so glossy, so full of swooping marble façades that are designed to seem old but were built only yesterday. I've hardly begun to understand this extraordinary palimpsest. You can lift up a corner of pavement and peer at a Mithraic temple. Shards and coins surface from Thames mud at low tide. Builders excavating rubble to dig foundations of new office blocks unwittingly become archaeologists, discovering the traces of Roman trading posts or burial grounds. The City heaves and contorts and gives birth to its past.

When you go for long walks through cities anything can happen. When you fall in love it's the same. You're not in control. When you walk around on your own you have adventures and meet strangers. Fear of going out is linked to fear of love. You might meet a stranger and fall in love. You might feel afraid that love is dangerous.

I'm sitting here in the bar feeling puzzled, a little light-headed perhaps. Light dances on the surface of my glass of Côtes du Rhône, sparkles on the long curve of zinc to my right across which the barman is sliding glasses of pastis for the waiter to load on to his round silver tray. I'm thinking of Pierre and I know I'm smiling. I'm not dreaming. But I don't understand what has happened. Since I'm carrying my notebook in my bag I can indulge myself, scribble down this account of what seems to have occurred in the last couple of hours.

I left the flat at three o'clock or so. I needed to get out and stretch my legs, and a walk seemed a better idea than a swim or a visit to the pub. I strolled north for a couple of blocks, turning right into Cheapside and then veering left up towards Liverpool Street. I had a vague idea of reaching Spitalfields market and buying some flowers and bread. Fool. I'd managed to forget it was Saturday and the food stalls are only there on Sundays. So I retraced my steps, meaning to return home by some pleasantly roundabout route. To wander down to London Bridge, perhaps, and back along the river towards Blackfriars.

I was thinking about love, how it creeps up on you and grabs you and knocks you out before you're aware of what's happening. Love the stalker. Love the mugger, the boxer, the bruiser. Love the poacher, setting you traps, throwing a net over your head and capturing you in a fierce grip. Love like a force of nature that cannot be checked, an avalanche, a mudslide, breaching your carefully built defences, flooding through you and possessing you. Love like a disease too: an infection, an obsession, a kind of madness, a wound, keeping you sleepless by night and restless by day.

Or – love like language, flowing out and surrounding the other, looping the loved one together with the self, cocooning you in shared stories and jokes. Fluent love. Love like a conversation that is endlessly renewed and renewing, a strong web that holds you up like a hammock. Love as the urge to talk, to tell the beloved everything that happens, to make life more real by drawing pictures of it for the other, your face turned endlessly towards his, wanting to give him all your words and receive all of his, wanting to create the world anew, pile his hands with gifts, wanting to give him yourself, it's that simple.

I'd stopped really noticing where I was going. My feet pulled me along as though they knew exactly my destination. I'd crossed the river, on to the south side, I'd gone past Sir Christopher Wren's house and was pursuing the path westward. I was vaguely aware of the grey December sky darkening and yet it was only mid-afternoon. A part of me remembered: yes, it's the day of the winter solstice, the shortest day. With my fur collar turned up and my hands thrust deep into my coat pockets, I strolled on.

I was thinking how women of my age were not supposed to fall in love. I had been a widow for ten years, very well, but now I was a grandmother, I had put away childish things, and certainly my four children, scattered across London, needed my maternal services as a regular babysitter, counsellor and good Samaritan. I was fortunate enough to be able to continue working as a photographer, I had several close men and women friends and many acquaintances and colleagues, I made just enough to live on, could afford to travel a bit if I budgeted carefully. My life was organized, busy and full, with no room in it for wildness or extravagance.

Besides, as I knew very well from what the culture shouted at me from every angle, every advertising hoarding, every TV programme, every cinema screen, old women were invisible and should stay that way. Worse, they were obscene and disgusting if they entertained thoughts of love and sex. Women past the menopause should cut their hair and retire from the field. They should not want physical pleasures, they should not have desires. Their ageing, sagging, unspeakably ugly flesh should remain hidden. They should not be occasions of shame and embarrassment to the young. And so on and so on.

Perhaps that was why my latest project had been to make portraits of people over fifty, both women and men. I photographed some of them naked and some clothed, according to the sitter's self-image on the day of shooting, according to our joint fantasy. I thought they were dignified, beautiful, angry, tender pictures but my children were not so sure. Pierre had liked the pictures I had pulled out of my bag and shown him, that first time I met him, when we had decided to have a coffee together in the Bar du Marché, he had written to say he liked the pictures I had sent him afterwards from London. And so of course I warmed to him. A man taking the time and trouble to look at what I had seen, to try to see things through my eyes, to gaze at my gaze, this pleased me. This was not vanity so much as gratitude. I don't usually expect men to see things my way, and am surprised and pleased when they do. No gallery had yet offered me a show, however, partly because other women photographers were perceived as already doing the same thing. My work was not original enough. Pierre liked my work, though. I could make something beautiful. That made me feel beautiful; that I had something to give. All of us need this validation from time to time I think, not only children. Pierre was a painter. He was fifteen years younger than I was. I fell in love with him in a matter of days. He didn't know anything about it. I had the sense to keep it to myself.

But love is a blessing, whether or not it's reciprocated, whether or not it's consummated, whether or not it can even simply be declared. Love had woken me up and made me want to work harder than ever, and make something more beautiful than I had ever made before. Love makes you feel you're being born all over again, catching you then swinging you by the heels in the air, that midwife love, laughing as you roar. And love also makes you humble as well as hopeful, realistic as well as mad. Men of Pierre's age don't fall in love with women of sixty. What would he see in me? I didn't think he'd laugh at me, he was too kind for that, at least he wouldn't laugh to my face, but he would be irritated, I was sure. He didn't need me to love him. He had plenty of love already, a young and beautiful lover. He'd shown me her photograph. Happiness and liking women generally made him charming to all the women he met, and I had fallen for his charm.

It was a fantasy. That was all. On to his handsome surface I had projected unconsciously the movie of my desire. I was using him. It was unreal. This was what I told myself fifty times a day. It will pass, Pauline, I instructed myself: it will dissolve, and go away eventually, and all you have to do in the meantime is keep a firm grip on yourself and not behave like too much of a ridiculous fool. I thought I sounded just like Charlotte Brontë berating her plain heroines for daring to fall in love with Mr Rochester, with Dr

Bretton. But at least Jane Eyre and Lucy Snowe were young. They
did have youth on their side. At least they had that.

I leaned on the parapet and looked at the Thames. The tide was
high and flowing fast. While I had been walking, the grey afternoon had been turning into glittering dusk; *l'heure bleue*. Now the
city swam in full darkness. Across on the other side of the river, the
edge between water and land was marked by loops of pearl lights,
long curving ropes of gleaming bulbs that swung a little, to and
fro, in the night breeze. Two barges were stationary in midstream,
providing a solidity and shape of blackness and mirroring shadow
beneath that contrasted with the light gleaming in long wavering
bands on the surface of the water. The far reach of the river was
black and purple rippled with dark green, and the nearer stretch
was indigo shot through with silver, streaked with gold-pink. The
barges rocked up and down on the tide, and their reflections
rocked too, shading out to triangles of black, and the lights poured
down on to the river in stripes of pearl and silver and gold and red.
More light glimmered in the dark sky, as the enormous moon
slowly emerged from enveloping clouds, strongly developing itself
like a photograph, warming to gold. This play and dance of light
and water was prodigal, an enchantment, it drew you into itself,
dissolved you into long dazzles of black river water streaming fast,
into moonlight and lamplight circling and glossy on the racing
tide. I had no camera. All I could do was stand and look.

I don't know how long I stood there. My face felt cold, and my
feet too, but I wasn't yet ready to return home. I was supposed to
be babysitting for one of my sons tonight, I remembered, and I
didn't want to. I thought I'd go and have a drink, and perhaps be

brave enough to phone my son and be thoroughly selfish and cancel babysitting. First of all, though, I had to find a pub. So I turned left, leaving the exquisite vision of darkness and light, the calm and emptiness of the riverside walk, and plunged down the first side-street I saw.

I walked rapidly, turning corner after corner at speed, skipping out of the way of passers-by. I was impatient, now, to be inside, somewhere warm. But I could see no pub ahead of me. When I turned, to retrace my steps, I hesitated, unsure which way to go. These little streets all looked the same, gay and enticing, hung with Christmas lights in the shape of snowflakes. One long, narrow tunnel of brightly illuminated shops led into another. For some strange reason, despite my familiarity with this bit of Southwark just east of Waterloo, I could no longer recognize where I was. I was lost. I had apparently strayed into some new development, some project of rebuilding and restoration that had happened overnight without my knowing anything about it. The stone façades of buildings were grey, cream, pale pink. Blue enamel signs, indicating house numbers, were nailed up alongside enormous wooden doors with smaller doors cut into them. Glass frontages displayed paintings and prints, new books, piled pots of *pâté de foie gras*, swathes of silk and velvet scarves. Everything looked delectable and expensive. Cars hooted as they tore past, taking little notice of pedestrians crossing the street, and poodles in gilt collars lifted their furry legs against the pillared entrances to boutiques while their ferociously chic owners tugged indulgently on their leads. There were a great many tourists around all chatting to each other in French.

I turned a corner. Now, at last, I found myself walking past a bar, whose wicker tables and chairs spilled out on to the pavement, and into a street market. I remembered the flowers and bread I had set out earlier to buy, and I slowed down.

The vegetable stalls were heaped with chestnuts, pumpkins and various kinds of wild mushrooms, while further along a butcher displayed fluffy white rabbits hung up by their heels, brightly feathered ducks and pheasants, legs of wild boar. A delicatessen offered tiny spinach quiches, so fresh you could see the nutmegged egg custard wobbling, the lightest of cheese pastry puffs, ham-stuffed mille feuilles and sausage rolls, a mouthwatering array of buckets of olives and pepper strips and artichokes in oil. I couldn't see a pub so I decided to settle for a bar. I turned and went back towards the one at the other end of the street, the Bar du Marché that I had passed earlier.

A discreet oblong sign, neat art-deco lettering on a faded mauve background, stopped me short. Hôtel Louisiane. There it was, exactly as I remembered it from all those years ago when I'd first started to visit Paris. A friend had recommended the Louisiane because it was cheap and also, more importantly, because Simone de Beauvoir had lived there once. I had stayed always on the fourth floor, in an austere little room high up under the eaves. The room contained a single bed covered with an orange chenille spread, a hard chair, a small Formica table under the high shuttered window. In the tiny adjoining bathroom was a threadbare towel and a minuscule bar of Lux soap. Across the street, when you stood on tiptoe and peeped out, was the *oeil de boeuf* window of the attic floor of the facing building. I would lie on the hard bed, daydreaming after my shower, waiting for my hair to dry, waiting for the next rendezvous with whoever it was, wondering if I'd ever meet Simone de Beauvoir's ghost.

If I was standing outside the Hôtel Louisiane then I was in the rue de Seine which meant I was in Paris.

I have come into the Bar du Marché and sat down near the zinc counter and ordered a glass of Côtes du Rhône. I am not asleep and I am not dreaming and I am not mad. I am in Paris. I am scratching this down, these black marks on this white paper. This is real.

The door opens and someone comes in from the street. He looks like Pierre. It is Pierre. When he sees me he smiles.

A FEAST FOR CATHERINE

for Giuliana Schiavi

The best days in Catherine's existence were the secret ones when she escaped to meet her lover Paul. They were her holy days. Sacred, because they let her escape daily reality and exist on another plane. Precious, because they occurred so rarely.

Being in love was like moving from black and white into colour. Like learning a new form of rejoicing which involved precise rituals of genuflection and praise. These evoked her Catholic childhood, those exact protocols of worship, the carefully orchestrated drama of the Mass, the particular liturgies and vestments that marked each important feast of the turning year. Being in love brought back the vanished, splendid days of Easter, when the cold church, masked and veiled during the penitential weeks of Lent, shrouded in darkness, burst forth in candlelight and organ music, in gold copes, in streams of incense, in baskets of perfumed lilies on the altars decorated with embroideries and lace. Year after year, without fail, in the springtime, Christ leaped from the tomb and the new fire blazed up and the rejoicing could begin all over again.

The many days that divided Catherine's fleeting visions of Paul were spent thinking about him, as she went about her tasks, in anticipation of their next encounter. These assignations could not be planned far in advance: Paul's life was too busy and complicated for that. Chances to see him turned up suddenly, like swallows diving past the house telling you it's summer. Catherine lived in a state of constant longing and of constant readiness. She prepared in advance for her possible absences. She kept the house very clean, and the freezer well stocked with food, and made sure she was always on top of the washing and ironing. So that if the possibility of seeing Paul occurred she could leave her husband and children without worrying too much. She could dash off at a moment's notice.

Paul would contact her every four months or so. Catherine would go to find her husband to tell him there was an emergency at work. She would call to him round the cowshed door, and he would grunt in recognition and assent, or she would holler at him across the field, and he would lift a hand in reply. She could rely on him, then, to be there when the two children got in from school, to give them their tea, and later on, if necessary, to see them into bed.

Catherine was a freelance translator of Italian commercial texts. Her husband had got used to her running up to London for last-minute meetings with editors and publishers. He didn't question these expeditions. If he wondered why her business had to be conducted face to face, in these days of e-mail and video conferencing, he didn't say. She had to make a living, after all. They needed the money she brought in. He relied on her for that.

The farm was always in debt. Catherine earned the money to pay the housekeeping bills and provide for the children. She took on extra translation work, of the sort she particularly disliked, car manuals and so forth, to finance her affair. Seeing Paul should not be at her husband and children's expense. She kept her love life on a separate budget and saved up for it in a secret account at the building society.

She wangled reduced-rate haircuts from trainees in the local salon. She picked up free samples of face cream from the cosmetics counter in the chemist. She hunted out cheap offers on lipsticks and nail-polishes and knew where to get good shoes at bargain prices. She hid these purchases along with the elegant clothes which she bought in the sales, hung at the back of her wardrobe, and never wore at home. She kept them for Paul alone. They should not come into contact with mud and dust, with cat hairs, with smelly dogs. They were pure and quiet. They waited, as she did. Occasionally she took out her pristine outfits and tried them on again. As she posed for the mirror she would think: if only Paul could see me in this. She was always on a diet, in order to be worthy of these clothes. For those few moments when he saw her she must remain slim. Love let you dwell in an eternal moment. She must not grow fat and middle-aged.

She had strict rules for her absences. She allowed herself to be away for a maximum of twelve hours. If she stayed in London overnight she was always home mid-morning the following day. She made it up to her children for not having been there to oversee their homework. She cooked her husband his favourite meal.

Now Paul had suggested a flying visit to Rome. His job as a communications consultant took him abroad all the time. On the coming Friday he had a breakfast meeting with some Italian telephone engineers, and at twelve noon he would meet Catherine at the Caffè Serena opposite the Pantheon. She could take the early-morning flight. She knew where the Pantheon was, didn't she? Yes, she did. It was round the corner from the church of Santa Maria sopra Minerva, where her namesake, Saint Catherine of Siena, was buried. She'd been there once before, when she was fourteen, on a trip with her convent school. Paul had rung off abruptly, just as she was telling him this, because someone had obviously just come into the room.

This trip to Rome was going to stretch the rules a bit. It would be complicated to organize such a lengthy absence from home. Two whole days. Expensive too. But it was the first time Paul had invited her on one of his business trips outside the UK and she didn't want to seem churlish and turn him down in case he never invited her again. She told herself it would be foolish not to go. She hadn't set foot in Rome since before the children were born. Working as a translator did not involve actually going to Italy. Everything could be done in front of a keyboard, a screen. She could not resist the idea of spending time with Paul in Rome.

She knew she would enjoy the journey itself. She liked going off on her own. no one knew where she was, and no one could get hold of her. She travelled on these occasions without her mobile phone. She could always ring home from a call-box if she wanted to. Mobiles signalled her professional efficiency, her domestic availability. They were not romantic. They lessened risk, took away your purity of intention. Not even for Paul, the telephone engineer, would she bring one of those chirruping instruments on a date. She trusted him to turn up. Trusting him was part of the delicious game, in which she handed him the power to make decisions. What a treat: to allow herself to be passive for once; not to be always responsible, adult, maternal, in charge. She could abandon herself; jump into the abyss and wait for the angel to bear her up on his wings. She could lie back and imagine herself a dandled child, rocked and tickled and caressed.

Her husband never tried to contact her while she was away supposedly working. He simply waited for her to return home. So she could go, invisible and loose, as light as air. She could vanish and get lost.

This time, she told her husband, she had been invited to a prestigious conference on translation. She would have to be away up in town for two days and nights. He was concentrating on the TV. He grunted. He'd be too tired, as well as too busy, to miss her much. The children weren't concerned either. They would be able to raid the freezer for pizza, skip taking baths, ignore the need to eat up their greens. She left on the dawn train for London and the airport.

She had forgotten what Italy was like. The difference hit her as soon as she stepped off the plane. It was probably something to do with the light. Hot, bright sunlight. Palm trees and sparkling air and the smell of dry heat – fruit, petrol, dust, flowers. Her black linen suit felt heavy. Why on earth was she wearing black? What a dull colour to choose. She took off the jacket and swung it over her arm. She was wearing a sleeveless yellow lace blouse. Now the warmth of the spring morning could caress her bare arms.

The airline bus dropped her off in the centre of the city. She found the Pantheon without difficulty. Its classical lines and curves were braced by scaffolding, its dome half veiled by sheets of plastic; it was closed for restoration. Catherine strolled across the oval piazza in front of it, surveying the cafés, their separate territories marked out by bright awnings, tubs of bay trees and orange trees. There was the Serena, its pavement patch set with silvery metal chairs and round tables draped with pink tablecloths.

She was much too early. It was only eleven o'clock. Time for an espresso, drunk standing at the bar. The café's interior was scented with vanilla and hot sugar and yeast. A wicker tray on the chrome counter was piled high with brioches studded with apricots, croissants scattered with slivers of almond. Her mouth watered, but Catherine reminded herself she was on a diet. She went out into the sunshine again, dawdled past the handsome fountain in the centre of the piazza, and strolled round the corner towards Santa Maria sopra Minerva.

Outside the marble-faced church two aproned women were paying their wet devotions to thresholds and steps with buckets and mops, sluicing streams of soapy water across the pavement. They smiled back at Catherine as she smiled at them, waving her apologies as she darted across their gleaming handiwork, trying not to leave footprints. She leaned her shoulder against the padded door, pushed it open. Inside, glittering darkness was cut with incense. Points of light were candle-flames, votive lamps. Gleams of sunshine, from slit windows, crystallized to carved amber. Here were the frescoes she remembered, that heavenly blue ceiling, those angels disporting themselves in red slashed sleeves and matching chic red sandals, those curly-haired blonde sibyls clasping scrolls and quill pens, revelling in their holy writing, those sweet-faced women disciples listening to Thomas Aquinas and shooting up their hands, earnest pupils eagerly denouncing the works of heretics, desperate to please the teacher and earn his praise. Catherine walked round, marvelling. Over and over again she fed 200-lire pieces into the slots in front of each of the painted chapels, to switch on the electric lamps and catch further glimpses of paradise.

In the largest side-chapel, behind an ornate iron grille, she rediscovered her namesake's burial-place. The life-sized wooden effigy of Saint Catherine of Siena had been lifted off the lid of her sarcophagus and placed across two trestles. Crouched over it, a young woman was sponging the statue's face, dabbing the lean cheeks with quick, deft gestures. The pots, bottles, rags and brushes of her trade were littered about nearby on the marble floor.

The statue seemed more than the image of the saint's dead, emaciated body. It seemed to be the corpse itself, stiffened by rigor mortis. It appeared to float in the chemical-smelling air, like an illusionist held up by a couple of fingertips in the old parlour trick. A tall lily was neatly disposed alongside, like a fairy's magic wand. Rosary beads like lumps of brown Demerara sugar were wound between the clasped hands. The saint's gaunt face was smiling though her eyes were shut. She looked as though she were merely asleep, dreaming of bliss. But she was dead. She was already in heaven. With Christ whom she loved.

Feeling she was disturbing the young woman restorer by staring so long, Catherine crept away. She waited at the Caffè Serena until past one o'clock. She built walls with sugar lumps and knocked them down. She gazed at pigeons pecking at crumbs and scraps. Paul wouldn't come now. She couldn't ring him; she'd deliberately left the number of his mobile phone at home. She didn't know the number of his hotel, or even the name of his hotel. She hadn't thought she needed to.

Saint Catherine of Siena had lived according to strict rules. She inhabited a framework of confinement, designed for her by others but embraced by her with eagerness. Perhaps that meant she couldn't spill out and be messy and dangerous, alarm the world with her cries of need, her raw red words of wanting and desperation. The thought of Christ contained her like a mother's arms. She could stay here for ever, rocked and hushed. He was milk, a cradle.

Saint Catherine of Siena was devoted to this lover she never saw, but in whose love and fidelity she believed utterly. She prayed to him without cease. Talking and telling, joking and playing. Though he remained resolutely invisible, though it was only faith, not proof, that let her believe her prayers reached him, she was convinced that she was in intimate communication with him by the sheer force of thinking about him every minute of every day. He hovered always round the corner, out of reach, and she lunged at him with her love and he dodged so that she lunged again.

She had kept everything that was best about herself for him alone. She had systematically deprived herself of food, so that she could transcend her body and try to be worthy of her unearthly paramour. She had gone hungry every day because he was all she needed and he had fed her with desire for him. She had come to Rome in pursuit of her great love and had died here, probably of starvation.

She was a madwoman, Catherine said to herself: just like me.

She went into the café's lavatory and wept with rage and humiliation, snorting and snivelling into her best Liberty handkerchief that she had bought cut-price in last year's January sale. She looked at her reflection in the mirror, red-nosed and swollen-eyed, and wept some more. Then she splashed cold water on her face, put on her dark glasses, and returned to her table in the sun.

The waiter arrived. He had curly fair hair and he smiled at her. Kindness to silly tourists: his speciality. She ordered a glass of white wine. It came, very cold, on a small silver tray. The first swallow was stingingly dry and icy. Sharpness flared in her stomach. She leaned back, listening to the splash of the nearby fountain, the church bells clanging out half past one.

Thoughts arrived like angels tumbling from the sky. She liked going off on her own and travelling by herself, didn't she? She liked vanishing from time to time, with no one at home knowing where she was. Had Paul just been an excuse for occasionally leaving home? Going off so that she could be sure she was choosing freely to return? She wasn't sure. But here she was, anyway. By herself, and no one in the entire world knowing what she was up to. She felt very light. Floating.

The waiter reappeared. He stood over her, licking the end of his pencil, lowering its wetted point to hover poised over his pad. With his tilted eyes and his long mouth curved into a smile he looked just like one of the sibyls on the ceiling in Santa Maria sopra Minerva. Perhaps the sibyls had been writing down recipes, orders for lunch? Catherine realized that the sharpness and lightness she was feeling spelled out hunger.

She ordered some more cold white wine, and a plate of mixed antipasti: slivers of fennel with olive oil and lemon, some slices of salami and prosciutto, a handful of black olives. She followed this with a bowl of *agnolotti* stuffed with mushrooms. Then she thought she'd like to try a side dish of artichokes, which she knew were a speciality here. Sipping her wine and peering at the menu, she couldn't choose between *carciofi alla romana*, stewed with tomatoes, or *carciofi alla judea*, deep-fried as crisp and golden as sunflowers. The solution was simple: she asked to be served both. She was feasting for two Catherines.

THE COOKERY LESSON

I began to love you when I met you in the flesh, as opposed to merely watching you on television, and first noticed your hands, their deftness and strength, your blunt-tipped fingers and very clean fingernails. On TV it was often only your face that the camera lingered over in closeup. Fair enough, because you are so beautiful, but I was frustrated; I wanted to see the rest of you and understand more intimately how you worked. I wanted to focus on how you dealt with gutting fish, preparing kidneys and liver, hooking the giblets out of ducks. But of course TV cooks aren't shown performing such acts; the audience might become upset at so much gloppy mess and blood.

Nonetheless, noting you insouciantly swirl crêpe mixture across your pan, give it just a second to set over the flame, then twist your wrist and flip the brown lace disc into the air, learning from your nonchalant demonstrations how to produce perfectly risen and crusted prawn soufflés and sweetbread-stuffed vols-aux-vents, I began to dream of meeting you.

I imagined it would be difficult to achieve this ambition. For years you'd run your own tiny restaurant in Kensington Park Road. But now, I discovered, you'd got fed up with chasing Michelin stars and had sold Chez Larry to a burger chain. You were no longer to be found, night after night, dishing up lobster *à l'Armoricaine* and tossing up your trademark towers of *foie-gras* mille-feuilles; you'd moved on. You were no longer readily available in public to your fans. Only on TV could you be spotted these days. You were a celebrity wrapped in privacy like a fillet of beef in pastry.

Then I read in a food magazine that you taught regular classes in the cookery school you had founded at your home in west London. Holland Park sang to me and summoned me. Number six Claridge Gardens said, come. I was a pilgrim with cocked hat, staff and sandal shoon.

Holland Park. Hang-out of women with crisply ironed striped shirts, collar wing-tips upturned above strings of pearls, gilt bars on their shoes, navy woollen tights, and wicker shopping baskets. *Palazzi* with Venetian-style windows and pastel plaster façades, elaborate wrought-iron gates. Tiny front gardens crammed with roses, wisteria and vines, jeeps and estate cars parked outside, expanses of communal green lawns at the back. Your house sparkled as though carved from sugar. A big white villa festooned with balconies, columns, cornices. I stood still for a moment, learning it. Then I trod reverently up the cream and grey marble steps and rang the bell.

Ten of us shuffled from the mirror-hung hall into the enormous, steel-clad kitchen in the basement, twitching our new overalls into place, adjusting our caps. We were not precisely beginners, having signed up for the Cordon Bleu class, but nonetheless we were nervous. You, my darling, didn't bother trying to put us at our ease. You were brisk and professional and just got on with the job. You shrugged at our clumsiness as we cracked eggs and dripped hot stock on to whisked yolks. You shouted at us when we dropped ladles or curdled our infusions of butter and meat juice. You gave us credit for not needing to be babied like the TV viewers and I liked you even better for it.

At the end of that first afternoon, I remember, you carved a chicken while we watched. How elegantly you dismembered it, parting muscle from bone with flicks of your razor-sharp knife, while we clustered around you and admired your unerring aim, your exactitude. So I fell in love, at that precise moment, with your hands, which knew just what to do. With your hands' capability and skill. And then with the rest of you.

When the class was over, I wove across Holland Park Avenue, dodging the rush-hour traffic, ran along Lansdowne Road with its Dutch-look houses, washed lemon, strawberry and sky, their long windows barred by grilles, crossed over Ladbroke Grove just below the lift of the hill, dived into Portobello Road. I got to the butcher's there just before it closed. The butcher I remembered so well from my squatting days in Talbot Road, before the landlords got rid of illegal tenants like me and the owner-occupier yuppies moved in. Breast of lamb or pie veal, that's what I ate on Saturday nights. Now the shop was decked with trussed game, rabbits hung up by their heels, strings of *saucisses de Toulouse*. I bought a free-range organic chicken and carried it home with me on the bus, nursing it on my lap like a baby, and poached it according to your recipe. Then I cut it up, just as you had, darting my knife into the tender joints. I ate it, every last scrap, thinking of you meanwhile. As though I were kissing your flesh and tasting you. I licked up lemon, tarragon, white wine and cream. Then I made stock from the bones.

I haven't got a proper kitchen here in Camden Road, only a shelf with a two-ring cooker and a tiny free-standing oven, and a small fridge underneath, but it doesn't matter. My kitchen, such as it is, has become transformed, like the rest of my life, by the power of love. My kitchen glows and is beautiful. While I cook I gaze out of the little dormer window, past the restless frieze of pigeons and seagulls strutting and pecking at the crusts I've put out for them on the sooty parapet of the roof, out over London rooftops. I can look westwards towards Holland Park as I patiently stir my bowl of thickening *sauce béarnaise* over a pan of bubbling water, or as I knead and pleat brioche dough, and think of you.

I'm making a chestnut pâté for supper tonight, no, not a nut roast, darling, what a tease you are, a proper pâté, composed of minced pork and veal mixed with crumbled chestnuts, bound with butter, flavoured with thyme and juniper berries, that I'll cook in the oven in a proper earthenware terrine I picked up cheap in Holloway Road car-boot sale because the lid is chipped, and I am making a proper tomato sauce, just as you taught us, with finely chopped celery, onion, parsley, carrot and garlic sweated in olive oil to start it off, to go with the delicious mound of scented chestnut-studded meat. Afterwards I'll serve a curly green salad tossed with a few roast hazelnuts and dressed with walnut oil, and a cone of goats' cheese. To finish: a plate of navy figs, that I picked out from my favourite stall in Berwick Street, the one with the man who sings out incomprehensible Cockney sales patter and tosses up the brown paper bags of vegetables by their twisted ears for the customers to catch. He'd make you laugh, darling. I'll take you there one Saturday and we'll buy purple-veined globe artichokes and thin *haricots verts* and then we'll go round the corner to Lina's and stock up on fresh *focaccia* and rocks of Parmesan and home-made pumpkin-stuffed ravioli. Arm in arm we'll wander along to the French pub in Dean Street for an aperitif, and then we'll have lunch at the Escargot before lugging all our goodies home.

Yes, you've guessed right, I wish you were here to eat this modest feast with me. Here in my little garret bedsit, perched opposite me by candlelight, smiling at me, smoking a Gauloise and drinking Ricard while I test the pâté with the point of my knife. I want to cook for you. I want to feed you the most exquisite dishes I can possibly make. That I learned in your class. That's one way of saying I miss you, now that the class has ended and I've found a temp job and I haven't seen you for weeks: to imagine cooking for you and to imagine writing this long letter to tell you so.

I was your favourite student because I was the most promising cook. You said I had talent. You singled me out for praise. All my life I had been so lonely and shy, so starving and desperate, and suddenly there you were, like the land of plenty, feeding me kind words, promises of affection, hints of a future together, perhaps opening a restaurant or sharing a new TV show. Even when you were brusque and gruff I could still feel the warmth simmering underneath. You didn't want all the others to know how you felt. Sometimes you stopped to chat after class but quite often you didn't. It was a signal to me, to warn me we had to be discreet.

I love you.

You haunt me. Whether I'm waiting at the bus-stop in the morning for the 253 to Tottenham Court Road or whether I'm home again in the evening, cutting carrots into julienne strips or simmering goose chunks for *rillettes* or perfecting my skimming of *sauce brune*, I'm aware of your presence. You're with me, in spirit, all day long. So I talk to you. The words bubble and run in my head and roll over my tongue like the blood gravy of *coq au vin*. If only you were with me here now and I could actually tell you all the things I feel. It is truly terrible not to be able to touch you. I caress the flesh of pork chops and calves' liver instead.

I dreamed of you last night, darling, as I dream of you almost every night. We were in company together, at a TV chefs' party of some kind, on the pavement outside the TV studios in White City, and then you turned your back on me and walked away. Please don't do that to me, darling. Can't you see it hurts? I don't think you understand how terrible rejection feels and that I can't bear the pain.

You see you light up my life and give it meaning. Before you came I had nothing and now you give me everything. London flushes with excitement, a suddenly magical city impregnated with images of you, inscribed everywhere with your name. As though all of London is your body, so that you surround me at every turn. As though you fly before me along these shabby streets, whistling just ahead of me around corners, leaving secret messages written in our private language for me to read. I translate the code of love on brick walls, uneven pavements. Paint splashes, chalk marks, graffiti. The tuft of feathery weed in the crevice of the neighbours' gatepost reminds me of your eyelashes. I saw your name – Spode – written up on a card in a china-shop window. The wholesalers in Old Compton Street sells checked chefs' trousers exactly like yours. Tonight the radio is playing songs from that *Paris Blues* CD I want to send you for your birthday. It's uncanny, how you are everywhere I look, how you drop these clues for me to find.

Tonight, remembering how you once told us in class you loved the *beignets* they make in those small, authentic bistros you can still discover in Paris, I have got out the deep-fat fryer because after supper I am going to practise cooking fritters. While the oil heats up I shall whisk together the batter of water, flour, one egg yolk, egg white, a dash of white wine. It's very light, not stodgy at all, the thinnest and crispest of golden coats puffing up in the smoking bath.

Those unlucky Christian martyrs tortured in vats of boiling oil – how ever did they bear it? I suppose God performed a miracle, saving them from feeling too much pain, to show how holy they were. I wouldn't want you ever to come to any harm, my precious one. Not the least touch of hot iron ever to blister your beautiful skin. If you were ever in danger of being harmed I'd rescue you. My love for you is certainly a miracle, because it makes me very brave and strong. There's nothing I wouldn't do for you and you know it.

Love is the power. So simple, isn't it? I cook well for you because I love you. Supposing you were here, supposing that you turned up after supper, very hungry, well, as an *amuse-gueule* I shall serve you deep-fried battered sage leaves, perfumed with just a drop of lemon, and deep-fried spoonfuls of egg white lightly mixed with grated Gruyère, fluffy golden clouds perched on tiny rounds of toasted baguette, and then afterwards deep-fried battered courgette flowers stuffed with minced mushrooms and chicken bound with cream.

London supermarkets these days are vast halls gleaming with treasure; even grubby old Holloway Road and Seven Sisters Road now have five between them, in which you can buy anything from anywhere in the world. The seasons no longer exist; time and space have been annihilated. Every whim can be satisfied, whether you want Korean red pepper paste and pickled cabbage, Mexican *mole* sauce of chocolate and spices, black *pastaciutta* dyed with squid ink, sesame-scattered Turkish loaves of bread as round and thick as your arm, or sweetmeats from the Lebanon dusted with honey crystals and flecks of brilliant pistachio. You've only to tell me your desire and I'll provide you with whatever you want.

I go shopping for you, my darling. I bring you home carrier bags full of gifts, spilling with scent and colour. Bouquets of emerald coriander and wreaths of pearly black grapes and alabaster curls of the very best *prosciutto* money can buy. I lug my sacks of food up four flights of stairs but I don't mind the weight. I fly upwards as though I were an angel, to my heaven-kitchen where you wait for me.

So what else can I offer you? After these rather rich delicacies that we started with, how about a good, bitter salad of red chicory leaves, and perhaps a slice of Camembert served on a toothed chestnut leaf, and then a dish of pears poached in spices and red wine? And of course if you were here with me I'd get out the very best Beaujolais in my cupboard. The two bottles I've been saving for a special occasion.

Wouldn't you like to come and eat these treats with me? Oh, please come and see me soon. Please ring me up. Please answer the telephone when I ring you. Please reply to my phone messages. Please acknowledge the gifts I post to you, and the e-mails I send you from work, desperately hoping my boss won't find out I'm using the computer to write love-letters not invoices. I take risks for you, darling, but love makes me reckless. Even if I got the sack for wasting the firm's time I wouldn't care.

I can't believe you don't love me as much as I love you. I know it's just that things are difficult for you right now. I do understand that. You've got to act cool, to seem to hold back. But in your thoughts it's a different matter. I've always been able to read your thoughts and I know how much you love me. It's just that at the moment you're not able to say. I understand that and I respect your attitude. Your message conveys itself to me through our special telepathy; mind to mind. On the surface you seem to behave with complete indifference but deep down inside I know you long for me.

It helps me very much to repeat all this quietly to myself while I fold shavings of pale cheese into egg white and test the heat of the oil with a crumb of bread, dropping it in then watching it turn rapidly gold. Rehearsing how I feel, well in advance of seeing you again, means my mind will be clear and calm when we do meet. I'll have cleared out all the junk and got rid of it, I shall be floaty and light as a fritter, friendly and normal, and you'll realize how much you do love me after all because you'll feel so good in my company. You won't be able to resist me.

You see I do know an awful lot about men, having observed them carefully, from a little distance, for, oh I don't want to admit for how long. I still feel just like a young girl inside. Because I haven't let experience sour or wither me. I'm still an optimist, an idealist even, and it shows on my face. Every morning when I'm putting on my makeup I look at myself in the mirror and tell myself how young I still look. My life can begin all over again. There's still time for you to admit you love me and for us to be happy together. We could move to Hampstead, we could buy a little Georgian cottage with a white-fenced garden and an apple tree and a kitchen just right for filming our cookery programme.

What I meant was, I know men don't like women to show too much emotion. You don't like it if we laugh or cry too much and particularly if we just do it and we haven't clearly explained to you why. You don't understand that if we could explain then we wouldn't be crying or laughing. But we appreciate you for being so clever and secure and successful and able to take everything so lightly. We rely on you for that.

With you I can relax and not worry about laughing or crying too much because you don't rub things in by discussing them. You and I are so close we hardly need to talk. We communicate through glances. I intuitively know how deeply you really love me.

Now, that's the problem with thinking too much while you cook. You almost burn things. I caught that sage leaf just in time. So I'm going to finish preparing supper, my angel, and then I'm going to open a bottle of Sancerre and eat. Please forgive me if I carry on talking to you, though, as I carry each delicious forkful to my mouth.

How I do love eating. Such bliss: the tastes of salt and hot olive oil coating this cloud of deep-fried egg white, the lightest of fritters, melting inside with Gruyère, each mouthful sliding over my tongue and down my throat, filling me up deep inside until at long last I am sated and can finally stop. Heavy with pleasure. Food like a sack of gold in my belly. My barn of harvest grain; my treasure store against the years of famine. I'll never starve again, for there is always more, as much as I want. I lick my lips, greased with olive oil, my lovely drug, the only one I need. It soothes me. I'd never be able to go on a diet and give it up. Olive oil tastes of summer and happiness and tranquillity and hope and love.

I used to be slim, as a girl, but I've become a plump woman, in fact I am what some people call a nice armful and others call fat. And yet I want to be more insubstantial than the paper of an imaginary letter, a ghost. Some people yearn to see ghosts but I yearn to be one. If I can't be with you, can't touch your arm as I talk to you, can't kiss and embrace you, then I'd like to nudge you in spirit instead. I want to be the invisible presence in the corner of your room, the object to which your thoughts obsessively return, the image you glimpse when you first open your eyes in the morning. I want to be there when you wake, and see you look at me.

Love has made me unashamed and bold. At first I contented myself with trying to catch a glimpse of you after work, getting off the tube in Notting Hill, walking down Holland Park Avenue and hovering about outside the posh bakery where I know you buy your croissants for breakfast the following day. Just on the off-chance that you might appear. Might spot me, greet me with pleased surprise, suggest we go for a drink. Somewhere intimate and quiet, with a certain bohemian charm, somewhere like Julie's Bar. I rehearsed what to say, what funny stories to tell you, anecdotes to amuse you. I had it all prepared, my conversation, to offer you like a fine dish of hors d'oeuvres *variés*, arranged with a flourish and served with a light hand, just as Elizabeth David says in *French Provincial Cooking*.

Then I grew more daring. I drew nearer to your house. I couldn't wait until dusk. I came to visit you in the mornings, before going to work.

I played fair. First thing, I went into Holland Park and had my potter, then did my meditation on the bench near the gate, so that if you'd been out for an early walk and encountered me on your way home it would have been a genuine accident, I'd have been able to say with perfect truth that I came here every day for exercise. Then, I strolled up and down the pavement outside your house, admiring the little bay trees in their terracotta pots adorning the steps, the ferns clustering to one side, the discreet iron hood over the cellar door. I was quite happily just waiting for you to wake up. Loitering with intent. To give you my love in person.

If you'd looked down into the street first thing yesterday, darling, when you got up, as you should have done, you'd have seen me there again, patiently attending on your pleasure, holding the bunch of mixed pink and red carnations and roses I bought for you in the twenty-four-hour supermarket next to the tube. But, without warning me first, you changed your signal. You changed your routine. You didn't draw the curtains, open the window and lean out to sniff the frosty autumnal air, as you've done all week. You didn't look out and spot me, as you usually do. I spied the lights go on behind the grey curtains – damask, I think, gleaming and heavy – but you weren't to be seen. In the end I was forced to leave the flowers on your front step. I hadn't got all day, my darling. I couldn't hang about waiting for you on the off-chance indefinitely. I knew you'd realize immediately the flowers were from me. Pink and red are your favourite colours, chopped veal awaiting its transformation into sauté de veau Marengo, and you know I'd never forget you telling me something like that. I walked through to Ladbroke Grove and ate breakfast in the greasy spoon at the corner of Elgin Crescent. Amazing it's still there, really, and not turned into a tapas bar. I celebrated the enduring nature of greasy spoons by ordering fried eggs and bacon, fried bread, sausage, mushrooms, baked beans, tomato, a side portion of toast.

I said to the girl who served me: that's a fry-up worthy of Larry Spode himself!

She looked a bit blank, then her brow cleared: oh, the bloke on telly, yeah, right.

Oh with what cunning I invent new ways to mention your name. At least once a day I gently insert you into my conversations with bus conductors, dry cleaners, my fellow clerks at work, and now the waitresses in greasy spoons. I thread you in like lardons into chicken skin before roasting. I rock you with my words, my darling, I hold you in the hands of my language, and I caress you with my tongue, all over. At the same time no one must suspect. It's my secret. Ours. You're my secret. My prisoner. I keep you captive inside my mouth and belly. I swallow you down with bites of mushroom and fried egg.

You're mine you're mine you're mine.

So, my darling, goodnight. Until tomorrow, then.

I'll see you even earlier than usual, long before you're expecting me. I'll tiptoe into your house by the cellar door under the front steps, which you carelessly left unlocked yesterday and whose key I was able to purloin, have copied, and replace, all in the space of twenty minutes. I don't like stealing and deceit, sweetheart, but you left me with no choice. You stopped communicating with me and thus threatened to deprive me of all I hold most dear: your love, my reason for living.

I can't stand rejection, being dropped into the bottomless black pit, where there is only the starving monster tearing with its fangs at its human prey, where there is only mouth and teeth and biting and death. You must not send me there, darling. I shouldn't be able to survive. Not after I have known this love.

So I'll creep into your bedroom while you're still asleep. I'll sit and watch you sleeping for a while. Then out of my handbag I'll take my Sabatier knife, the one you recommended, that I use for carving. You won't need to be afraid. You won't feel a thing, I promise you. I'm your apt pupil. I shall be accurate. I shall be swift. I'll hold you in my arms and kiss your beautiful hands and then I'll cut you up and cook you and eat you and we'll never be parted again, oh no nevermore, my sweet angel, you'll be mine for ever and you won't be able to leave me, darling flesh of my flesh, not this time, oh no never again.

LISTS

October 1st

Start to plan Christmas menus. Venison? Goose?

Supermarket.

Rake leaves from orchard.

Buy daffodil bulbs.

Speak to Father Dan about changing flower rota.

Speak to Cedric about his snoring problem.

Drycleaners – my silk suit.

Look thro Chr. catalogues for presents for the girls.

October 7th

Rake leaves and keep for mulch.

Start new slimming diet.

Supermarket extras: low-fat marg., low-fat fromage frais, low-fat
mayonnaise, sweeteners, bran.

Invite Father Dan to dinner this week.

Minutes for Women's Inst. meeting next week.

Ring the girls about their Christmas plans.

October 14th

Raking, mulching, pruning.

Ideas for Christmas décor. A small Christmas tree in every
room? Great swags of greenery laid over the mantelpieces?
NB get book from library on Renaissance palaces, gardening,
etc.

Whist drive at church. Do sandwiches.

Supermarket: large tubs of low-fat cottage cheese.

School governors meeting. My silk suit? Hat?

October 21st

Cedric's snoring: mention herbal pillows as a possibility? *Gently.*

Resolve keep up *positive* approach!

Order Christmas presents for Sophie and Angela from
catalogues.

Check bank statement again. Check with Cedric?

Finish bagging leaves for mulch.

Christmas trees. Use the medium-sized ones from bed in kitchen
garden? Yes. Check holly, mistletoe.

Aerobics class.

Church cleaning rota. Mention can't come this week.

Mention to Father Dan I'll provide all greenery for church
Christmas decorations.

Supermarket: low-fat plain yoghurt.

November 1st

Yeast pills.

Spring clean – autumn clean!! – guest rooms for girls' visit this coming weekend.

Take Hetty to vet. Father Dan says fleas but can I be sure? Check with vet.

Ring council about caravan parked in lay-by next to church. Gypsies?

Make appointment with GP for Cedric.

Buy large sacks compost, peat, lime.

Talk for Young Catholic Mothers group. Tweed suit?

Silk suit to cleaners.

NB special offer of tinned chestnuts in supermarket. Stock up for stuffing. *None* for me of course!!

Search diet recipe book for low-fat stuffing recipe.

Cancel Cedric's GP appointment and make one for me. Resolve to stay *calm*. Do *not* get angry with Cedric. Snoring minor problem really.

November 7th

Buy relaxation tapes Sophie told me about on phone.

Ring Sophie and Angela back and suggest another weekend for visit. Mustn't harass them! Just come for Christmas? What about New Year?

Suggest to Cedric he could try hypnotherapy for snoring? NB Angela's good experience with nailbiting. Be *tactful*.

Plant bulbs in garden.

Buy extra compost.

Plant extra bulbs in pots as extra Chr. prezzies for those
    unexpected visitors!

Buy squared paper. Do design for garlands on hall banisters,
    wreaths for doors, swags for mantelpieces.

Do designs for festoons around crib in church, vases on altar,
    hanging baskets in nave.

Cleaning rota. Can't do this week.

November 14th

Supermarket: celery, low-fat milk.

Buy three hundred stamps for Chr. cards.

Check store cupboard for ingredients for Chr. cake, pudding,
    mincemeat.

Substitute cottage cheese for suet? Check with Sophie when
    asking about her Chr. plans.

Go to confession.

Invite Father Dan to Chr. drinks.

Buy gold braid, gold paint, silver paint, glue, corrugated paper,
    tissue paper, crêpe paper, gold paper, silver paper, gold and
    silver stick-on stars, gold and silver string, white cartridge
    paper, white cardboard, gold glitter, silver glitter.

Get out fir cones, dried flowers, dried thistles and grasses.

Wire.

Start novena to St Jude about Cedric's snoring.

November 21st

Jiffy-bags, brown paper, airmail stickers, staples, stapler. Post all
    presents for abroad.

Make Christmas cards.

Make pudding, mincemeat, cake.

Invite Father Dan to tea. Mention I'm only too happy to take
  sole charge of Chr. decorations in church.

Aerobics!

December 1st

Suggest separate rooms to Cedric just as temporary measure
  while I recover from last week's collapse. Stay *calm*.

Renew library book on Medici palaces and gardens.

Weedkiller?

Cleaning rota. Mention I still feel too weak.

Knights of St Columba Ladies' Night Dinner Dance – check
  gold shoes, handbag. Send balldress to cleaners. Write speech.

Order goose from butcher.

Find recipe for goose *rillettes*.

Substitute cottage cheese for goose fat?

Buy boxes of crackers, oatcakes, Earl Grey tea, cranberry jelly,
  champagne, sherry, gin, brandy. Wine.

December 7th

Confront Cedric over blank stubs in joint account chequebook?
  His Christmas presents to me and the girls?

Resolve to try to be more trusting.

Go to confession.

Give talk to Women's Institute on dried flowers and grasses
  arrangements for Christmas lunch-table centre-pieces.

Buy exercise bicycle, new leotard, sweatbands, workout video.

Attend primary school nativity play with other governors. Silk suit, hat.

December 14th

Book Hetty into kennels for New Year.

Book airline tickets, hotel in Rio. Travel insurance. Check passport.

Wrap Christmas presents for Cedric and the girls.

Post all Christmas cards.

Finish making all Christmas decorations.

Get out damask tablecloth and napkins and check.

Buy candles for tree, wreaths, table.

Try massage for migraines?

Go to confession.

Primary school carol concert. Tweed suit.

Silk suit to cleaners.

December 21st

Make canapés, pâtés, dips, croûtons, for Christmas drinks party. Bridge rolls, cocktail sticks, cocktail napkins, cocktail sausages.

Decorate church with lots of lovely old-fashioned holly and ivy and mistletoe from the garden.

Decorate house ditto.

Organize primary-school children's carol-singing house to house.

Dig up twelve small Christmas trees from bed in kitchen garden and decorate.

Ring Angela and Sophie back and wish them a happy Christmas with their boyfriends' families.

Try one last time to convince Cedric of health dangers of
snoring: lack of oxygen!

Buy disposable syringe.

Look forward to Christmas!

December 30th

Inject Cedric with fatal air embolism while asleep snoring after
lunch.

Dispose of syringe and plastic gloves.

Get Father Dan to help me move corpse to prepared trench in
bed in kitchen garden. Cover with lime, then with compost
and peat. Replant Christmas trees on top, mulch well with
prepared rotted leaves. Plant a few bulbs here and there.

Take Hetty to kennels.

Put away Christmas tree decorations.

December 31st

Leave for airport with Father Dan. Silk suit, no hat.

January 1st

Make New Year's resolutions: try to tackle this obsession with
lists; help Dan choose title for article for the *Tablet* on why
he's leaving the priesthood; start novena for Cedric's soul.

BLATHERING FRIGHTS

A NOVEL IN THREE CHAPTERS

for Paul Bailey

CHAPTER ONE INSPIRATION STRIKES

May I come and join you? You looked so lonely standing over there in the corner clutching your drink in your hot little hand. You must be Solange. And I'm Cathy. With a C.

You writers do drink an awful lot, don't you! Don't you ever worry about your liver? You're not feeling nervous, are you? Not of poor little us, surely.

We've just come to sit at your feet and drink in every word!

It is a lovely garden, isn't it? Of course you won't have had time to see over it yet. You've only just arrived. And quite the most important thing is getting yourself a drink! Now you can relax. I'm sure you'll love it here.

Oh yes, I've been coming for several years now. There isn't an inch of the place that I don't know. I've been on some marvellous courses here. With some really wonderful tutors. The poetry course I was on last time, with Greg Thunderbottom, well. That was something. He really knew how to give. Of himself, totally, and of his expertise, and of his time. It wasn't a large group course like this. It was more intimate. More like a retreat. We went off into the woods, or up into the hills, to write, and then one saw him every day, alone, for an hour. Such precious times, those hours with Greg. He knew how to listen. He knew how to draw out one's soul. It's impossible to put into words.

Oh, you've met him, have you?

Don't you just adore his books? Such strength, such confidence. But such gentle authority. We got very close, actually. I felt he really understood my work, my struggles. Such a shame he decided not to tutor a course this year. I was so looking forward to working with him again.

And so what do *you* write? I must confess I haven't read any of your books. What are they about? You have published more than one I suppose?

You'll have to excuse me asking all these questions! It's so exciting meeting a real writer, not just a scribbler like oneself. Though I'm afraid I must admit I'd never heard of you before signing up for this course. Who is your publisher?

Oh, I see.

And have you had much experience of teaching creative writing?

Greg of course is a really wonderful writer. I'll lend you one of his books, if you like. I brought them all with me in case some of the other students needed something to read. I bring all sorts of things with me on these courses, you never know what will come in handy.

Dictionaries, of course, rhyming dictionaries and *Roget's Thesaurus*, and then I've got this lovely little book Greg wrote about how to teach creative writing. I'll lend it to you, if you like. It might give you some inspiration for tomorrow.

Oh, you've already planned the morning workshop, have you? How terribly organized you must be. I'm afraid creative chaos is more my line! I'm not very good in groups. It reminds me of school, and how much I suffered there. You mustn't mind if I don't seem to be paying attention in the workshop tomorrow. My inner life is so demanding. Sometimes my mind just wanders off and I'm lost to the world. You mustn't be hurt if I don't join in the exercises you get the others to write. I find all that sort of thing a bit mechanical. A bit artificial. I prefer to write when I'm outside, sitting in a meadow or perched on a boulder in the middle of a stream, not in a room with fifteen other people. So if I nod off in the workshop you mustn't mind.

It's just that I'm awfully sensitive. The slightest thing is enough to set me off. Perhaps you and I could meet on our own tomorrow afternoon? I'd like to show you the sonnet sequence that I wrote when I was working here with Greg last year on that lovely poetry course I was telling you about. It's tremendously sexual of course, very savage yet very controlled. It's about my inner animal. It's called *Bear*. I asked Greg to send it to his agent, but Greg said it was too avant-garde, too experimental. He didn't think the poetry world was quite ready for it yet!

Oh, you write free verse do you Solange? You don't think that's kind of cheating somehow? You must show me your poems some-time.

I love the discipline of form, somehow. Villanelles. Last year on the poetry course we used to play games after supper and I was always begging for us to write villanelles. I find so many modern writers don't actually know a great deal about poetic form.

Do *you* know what a villanelle is, Solange?

You do?

Greg, I'm afraid, felt forced to be gently deprecating about many of our women poets. So many of them, he would say, wrote in a way that lacked virile force and muscular edge. I used to tease him about it. You're a Titan among men, I used to say to him: you can't expect us all to live up to you!

He's so *big*. Great hulking shoulders. Burning eyes. And of course his soul is really enormous too. He doesn't really need to teach, of course. He doesn't need the money. He does it for love. And what was wonderful was that he let one give something back. Sympathy. Understanding. As soon as I'd finished my villanelle sequence *Forest of Blood Forest of Bone* on the course last year I rushed up to his room to read it to him, and even though it was midnight he lay there and listened.

Writing's such a solitary business, isn't it? I intuitively felt Greg's deep loneliness. His need of a kindred spirit.

There's something about that electric charge between men and women, the creative spark I call it, between sexual opposites, that clash of attraction, Dionysian thingy anima-animus, well, when it happens, there's no point denying it. You have to yield.

Greg, of course, being such a great poet, with such an unusual soul, understood women completely. He could be as simple as a little child. He'd just gaze at you. His penetration into the feminine heart was quite amazing. And he could be so maternal too. The first day of the course, I remember, I was suddenly overwhelmed by angst. Everyone else was drinking wine and writing limericks, rather superficial stuff I'm afraid, and I suddenly burst out weeping. I felt so vulnerable, so in need of comfort. I rushed out into the garden into the rain. And then when all the others had gone to bed, I went to find Greg to borrow a towel to dry my hair with, you can see what long hair I've got, I was simply drenched, and Greg poured me a whisky and suggested I write a poem about the wild, wet garden, and my feelings. And that was how I began *Forest of Blood Forest of Bone*. I dedicated it to Greg. I used to read it out in our work-in-progress workshops, as the week went along, and I'm afraid some of the others got terribly jealous. They minded the way that I found this transitional, special psychic space on the stairs to Greg's room, where I used to sit and work. I'm afraid some women have petty minds. I'm afraid sometimes there is rather an unhealthy element of competitiveness on these courses. Women vying with each other to get the tutor's attention. Keep him all to themselves.

It's so lovely, Solange, that I'll have the chance to work with a woman this time. I've never met a lesbian before. I hope you don't mind my saying that. May I get you another glass of wine?

CHAPTER TWO PUTTING DOWN ROOTS

Hello. Do come in.

Yes, it's marvellously tranquil here. With the bleak wild moors

all around, and the only sound the cry of the curlew and the purl-
ing of the beck, well, you can see what inspires me, can't you?

Yes, less so in summer of course, with the hordes of tourists
tramping through, but I don't want to complain. We are all souls
in search, are we not, all fumbling our way up the one mountain?

Yes, of course this is moorland country. I meant mountains in
a spiritual sense. I spoke metaphorically.

Yes, very unlike London. I lived there for some years, and I'm
afraid it was soul-destroying. The effect it had on people. Too
much spite and gossip. Backbiting. Certain people were extremely
unkind to me. I think they were envious of my success. It quite
poisoned the atmosphere. So we decided to move up here, to
somewhere quieter and more peaceful, with room to breathe.
Solange missed the restaurants and the good delicatessens at first,
but in fact she has turned that to her advantage, as you see. I have
nothing to do with running the wine-bar, of course, but she likes
it. It gives her something to do, and it provides us with a stable
income, which we badly need. The reading public can be so capri-
cious!

No, I don't miss London at all. I found so few kindred spirits
there. Londoners, and writers in particular I'm sad to say, can be so
coarse, so unfeeling. People wrote such horrid things about me.
They were trying to shut me up. It was bullying, in fact. It was a
form of –

Oh, your machine appears not to be working, does it?

No, no, not at all. My time is yours. Perhaps, while we wait, you
would like another cup of herbal tea? Just let me call Solange
and –

Oh, it's working now, is it? You're sure it's actually working now?

Oh, the little red light. Oh, I see. I'm afraid I'm hopeless with machines. I've always felt that *proves* I belong to an earlier age.

Well, of course, Solange has her little jeep. It's really handy for the shopping. Once a week she drives into Haworth and brings back all our supplies. She's got a huge freezer out the back, a couple of microwaves, she's very organized.

Me? Heavens, no. I'm a bit of a recluse, I'm afraid. Walking the moors at all hours with the wind blowing in my hair, singing my wild, shy songs to the skylarks and the sheep, then coming home and writing my novels, I'm afraid that's all I'm good for!

Yes, Solange did fancy herself as a bit of a writer once. How funny you should have remembered that. But once she discovered her true vocation she stopped her scribbling and has become tremendously happy.

Yes, I am fortunate. Solange is the only person, apart from a few Brontë scholars, who can read my crabbed, minuscule writing. My scrawl, as she calls it. She's remarkably gifted in a practical way. People who lack imagination often are, have you noticed? I can hand her a whole stack of pages in the afternoon, rather cramped and full of crossings-out and blots, I'm afraid, but when Emily comes through and takes possession of me and I go into trance, well, Emily dictates so *fast*, and she insists I write very small just like she did, so, in the evening, after Solange has closed the wine-bar, she just whips out the word-processor, and by the next morning there's a beautiful neat pile of A4 pages, all collated and double-spaced and everything, ready for me to correct.

Yes, I founded the Brontë Press with the money from the divorce. Little enough as there was. Men can be such brutes. Such brutes! Thank heavens I discovered my true sexuality when I did. There is such tenderness, empathy, sensitivity and deep communion between women, men envy it I'm afraid. They seek to destroy it. My ex-husband simply could not understand my needs. Nor could he understand my poems. When I left him and the children to move up here with Solange, he divorced me as fast as he could. Poor man. He'd met another woman, some pathetic, deluded suburbanite taken in by his poor-little-boy act. Men are such children, I'm afraid. So lacking in fine feeling. Not you, of course. I can't tell you how delighted I am that you want to write your Ph.D. on me. I am so moved by a young person taking such an interest. I was so delighted when you wrote to me.

Yes, Solange answers all my letters. I must admit I receive sackfuls of fanmail, all these desperate would-be writers asking my advice, oh, she's my right hand. She loves being kept busy. It gives her less time to brood over that unfortunate business on Hampstead Heath just before we left. It frees me to get on with my work, serving Emily Brontë, and of course that is the most precious thing in life. To both of us.

You hadn't quite realized what?

I was coming to that. In my own good time.

Yes. I have discovered I am a reincarnation of Emily Brontë. She is my muse and my spirit guide. *She* is *me*.

Yes. It is amazing, isn't it?

I must admit that for a time I wasn't sure that I wouldn't be Virginia. The prose pouring out of me, after that wonderful writing course where I met Solange, was so remarkably Woolfian. And Solange does in fact bear an astonishing resemblance to Vita Sackville-West. But then, after we got free of Hampstead and its rather clogged literary atmosphere, and I began to breathe a purer and loftier air than the metropolis could provide, it all became clear. We were sitting in First Class, I remember, sipping gin and tonics, and I heard this voice distinctly say: Cathy, you *are* Heathcliff. So then I knew. I *was* Emily Brontë.

That was it. No turning back. And so my androgynous theory of literature was born.

Well, you see, once you realize that essentially Heathcliff is a lesbian –

Oh dear. Never mind. I don't think tea with goat's milk stains as badly as the ordinary kind. What a pity your trousers are white. Most Branwellian!

You wanted to know about the scene on Hampstead Heath? Far be it from me to spread malicious rumours about people. I will say only this. When I was confronted, at the Ladies' Pond, by a madwoman purporting to be Greg Thunderbottom's wife screaming at me that I had ruined her marriage, of course I had to protect Solange, who was standing with us on the diving-board at the time.

No, of course I didn't know Mrs Thunderbottom couldn't swim. Naturally I was very upset. I wrote a sonnet sequence called *Weeds* which I sent to Greg. I thought it could have been read aloud at the funeral. And then what did Greg do but go into print shortly afterwards, on the *TLS* letters page no less, accusing me of plagiarizing his work for my epic poem in *terza rima Dark Deeps*.

I was bruised. Shattered. So we came here. To be blessed by Emily. And to open Haworth's first women-only wine-bar.

Yes, that is indeed a pair of early nineteenth-century riding-boots over there in the corner, and that is indeed a pair of silver spurs, and that is indeed a whip. To you, dear Henry, I may call you Henry I hope rather than that awfully formal Mr Grapple, they may well suggest a souvenir of Heathcliff, but Solange and I both know they are Branwell's.

Yes, of course I will explain.

Well, once you understand the androgynous nature of litera-ture, of great art in general I should say, it becomes obvious that no ordinary mere feminine heterosexual woman, thinking of nothing but silk frocks and vaginal orgasms, could have written *Wuthering Heights*. And so Emily is adamant that, for the sequels, there must be something transcendentally virile about the writing. So, when-ever I get a little weary, and can't hear Emily's voice as clearly as I need to, Solange puts on the boots and her jodhpurs and the spurs and whips me on!

Yes, I said whips. I spoke metaphorically.

Yes, she *becomes* Branwell. And then, oh then, Henry, I don't need to tell you what happens next. The words rise up and pour out. And I am humble. I am grateful. I weep and write.

CHAPTER THREE BLISS

Hello, padre. Do sit down. This bunk is not too hard once one gets used to it. So kind of you to call. As you can see, I am always at home!

I love the austerity of this place. This pure, white enclosure. All my life I have written about inner space and now, at last, I inhabit it. No, I am not filled with bitterness and rancour. Why should I be? I have endless time to meditate, to think and read, to pray.

You see, padre, my whole life has been a quest for truth and meaning. And here, in Holloway prison, I have been granted my vision. I have discovered that I am not bisexual, as Solange accused me of being before she unfortunately succumbed to food poisoning, but celibate. I want nothing, now, but to sit here and feel myself empty of all passion, all desire, all that greediness and grabbing that people out in the world inflict on each other.

It's like a monastery in here, padre. I think of my cell as my cell.

I am happy. I am calm.

Oh yes, I have been vilified. I have been accused of terrible crimes. I faced my accusers from the dock and silently forgave them.

You want to know what I was accused of? Oh padre, it will make you smile to hear how an ordinary, innocent, simple woman such as myself could be imagined to be so evil.

Well. Let me remember. Various murders, of Mrs Thunderbottom and Solange and her secret paramour Henry Grapple, oh yes and my ex-husband and my three children who all got food poisoning too, and if that weren't enough, embezzlement, theft, plagiarism and I don't know what else on top. People have been very cruel, I'm afraid.

Yes, padre, I have survived. Because my mind to me a kingdom is. I sit here and I recite poems to myself, all those poems I wrote before they were taken away from me and declared the property of others. I think about Marie Antoinette, so noble and dignified in her last days, filling her dank apartment in jail with the scent of regal courage. And of course I write. Thanks to the little creative-writing group I run here, I have received so much encouragement and support that I am able to go on. I'm not worthy, of course, to lead the group, but the others insisted. I have, after all, suffered so much more than they. The atmosphere, when we read out our work, becomes quite electric. Sometimes I think of the suffragettes. At other times I think of the martyrs of the early Church.

Oh, you're not going yet, surely? Do please stay a little longer, padre. I was hoping we could pray together. And then I thought you might like to hear the opening chapter of my autobiography. I began writing it just before poor Solange died, just after that detective inspector pretending to be a graduate student came into my life and ruined everything. He seduced Solange, you know. She was such an innocent, she knew nothing about men. I couldn't let him stand in our way. I had to protect Solange. I knew that, deep down, she gave me permission to do what I did. When Henry Grapple took ill on that fateful afternoon, I knew that Solange, if she hadn't been dead already, would have insisted that I finish my chapter before calling the ambulance. And of course she was right.

Greg too, he always insisted that art must come first. I wrote a very beautiful poem for his funeral. It was called Deep Darkness.

Now that they're all gone, poor things, I've discovered that there's just one person who really understands me, really loves me. God. And that, dear padre, is the reason I asked you to come here today. I want to say thank you to the universe, whose rhythms I feel pulse inside me as God dictates fresh poems, fresh chapters of my life-story!

Fine, padre, fine. Of course I understand.

I look forward to seeing you next week.

THE EASTER EGG HUNT

My little brother was born two weeks before Easter and I hated him. My hatred was scarlet, and twisted inside me like a plait, and snapped in my mouth like the metal brace I wore on my teeth. My hatred felt as ugly as me when I looked in the mirror. That's why they had a new baby: because I wasn't sweet any more, couldn't be doted on. I was ugly and clumsy and made too much noise.

They sent me off to stay with Mémé and Pépé so that I'd be out of the way now that the new baby had been born. At first they were going to send me to be a boarder at school, because Pépé had been ill and they didn't want me to be a nuisance. Luckily for me the nuns didn't want me around, because it was the holidays, with all the other girls gone home, and Holy Week was coming up, with all the extra praying they had to do. So Mémé said I should go and stay with them like I always did at Easter, she was sure I wouldn't be any trouble.

She put me to bed that first night in the room I always slept in when I was staying. It was *my* room. The wooden bed had curled-over ends. Sleeping inside it was like being in a boat. When you sat on the edge of the bed your feet couldn't touch the ground. The sheets smelt of fresh air, from being dried outside, not in a machine, and they were thick and rough, with a long seam down the centre, from being turned sides to middle once they'd worn out, and square patches to cover the holes. They were plain greyish-white, not like the flowery yellow ones we had at home. There were no flowered curtains either, just a blind with a cord you pulled to make the blind fly up. The window had an egg-shaped knob you twisted, and then both sides of the window pushed out like doors and you could smell the farmyard: hay and manure.

I could feel the cold shape of the window-knob inside my fingers even when I was back in bed falling asleep. It reminded me of Easter eggs wrapped in gold and silver paper. On Easter morning, after we'd come back from Mass, I always had my Easter egg hunt in the garden. Pépé said it was the Easter Rabbit who left the eggs for me but of course I knew it was him. Every year he hid them for me, in harder and harder places to find. This year he was ill. Or he might have forgotten.

My father had driven me over to Mémé's house in a hurry, driving very fast so he wouldn't waste any time getting back. Promise me to be good, he said to me in the car: help Mémé, don't answer back, remember Pépé's been very ill, don't *create*.

In Pépé's and Mémé's house I'd thought I'd be safe, but that very first night, I saw the devil.

He flew past the house. Scaly leathery wings he had, like a bat, and a shiny breastplate like a beetle, and furry feet with claws for toes. His eyes were glittering and red like pieces of ruby and his mouth was wide and thin, curved into a smile.

The owls hooting woke me up. There aren't owls where we live, so I'd forgotten what they sound like. That strange wobbly call, like a breath blown into a flute, long and cool and trembling, repeating itself over and over again. Very close to the house. I sat up in bed and saw that the blind had come loose at the bottom and rolled itself half-way up the window, letting in the white moonlight.

I got up and went over to the window and looked out through the pane of glass not covered by the blind. I was hoping to see the owls, but I saw the devil instead. There he was, about as tall as me, standing on the orchard gate. I knew it was him because he looked exactly like his picture in my book of Bible stories at school. His hands were crossed in front of him and his head was bent. Considering. He was like the owls. Choosing what to hunt and kill next.

He was looking for me. I thought if he didn't see me he might think he'd made a mistake, I wasn't there after all. I took a step backwards, and put my hand on the edge of the blind, wondering if he'd notice if I tugged it down. He was so still, like the buzzards Pépé used to point out to me hovering above the fields, waiting to spot their prey and swoop down on it.

Then the dog began barking, at the front of the house, and it startled him. He straightened himself and stretched, with a clatter, as though he was made of metal and stone. He rose up in the air, the stars peppering his wings and the moon his hat. He flew off, across the orchard, round the far corner of the house, and vanished. The dog had smelt him and warned him off.

I unlatched the door of my room and went into the kitchen. The ash in the hearth glowed red. I felt my way along the table that ran through the centre of the room, running my hands over the wooden chairs pushed close in for the night. The darkness in here was friendly. Not all darkness was like that. Recently in my room at home things had started to come out at night and try to frighten me. Hands stretched through the keyhole, skinny fingers with knuckles as knobbly as roots tried to stroke the back of my neck, mouths blew cold air down my ear while I lay with my eyes tightly shut and the bedclothes clutched round me. I called these things *IT*. Now I knew that *IT* was the devil. He had followed me here. I didn't want him to find a way into Pépé and Mémé's house.

I could hear the clock ticking on the mantelpiece and the mice scampering about in the roof, and the rafters creaking. Outside the owls hooted again, and the dog growled. Pépé was snoring so loudly I heard him through the wall. His snores were a cross between gulps and gurgles. I heard the bedsprings creak and Mémé get up. Their door opened and she came out and found me standing there.

– What's the matter? she said: had a bad dream?

She shuffled across the room, kicking her feet into her mules, yawning and doing up the belt of her dressing-gown. She reached down and took hold of my hand.

– You'll catch your death, she said: standing about in bare feet. Come on, we'll sit in the armchair for five minutes and then you must go back to bed.

At night Mémé was so soft, without her girdle on. She was a bulk of warmth I burrowed into once I was curled up on her lap with my feet tucked down the side of the chair under a cushion. She put her arms round me and her chin on the top of my head. She smelt of face cream and talcum powder and bed. At night she was gentle sometimes. In the daytime she was often cross and snapped at everyone, Pépé included, because she had so much to do, too much work for one pair of hands she would shout, and everyone wanted her to help them all the time, until she flung up her hands in the air as though she was going to hit you. It was the way she was. She was fierce like her big dog outside, suddenly barking. Then she'd dash off and it would be over, like a storm of rain.

The dog was quiet now. He'd heard Mémé get up, so that he knew that all was well. He'd be lying down again, on the top step, just outside the door, head between his paws.

Mémé said into the top of my head: tomorrow afternoon, that's today really, we'll phone up and see how your little brother's getting on. D'you think he's missing his big sister?

She expected me to say something grown-up and polite but I wouldn't. Everyone kept telling me I was a big girl now, and I hated it. I could feel myself wanting to cry, but the tears came out as words. I couldn't stop them.

– I want you always to love me the best, I said: not him. Now he'll be your favourite not me. I want to be the one you love the most.

She pinched my earlobe then slapped her hand very lightly against the side of my face.

– Oh my bad girl, she crooned to me: my bad, bad grand-
daughter.

I stuck my thumb in my mouth and lay back against her. She
hugged me tight, and stroked my hair, and waited for me to grow
sleepy. After a bit she pulled my thumb out of my mouth, hoisted
me down, gave me a push, and shooed me into bed. She was just
the same with the animals, so I felt content. When she wanted the
animals to move, she'd give them a tap, then a shove. The cows, for
example, at milking time. Very quickly she'd lose patience, then
she'd grab a switch and hit them on the flank, until they lumbered
off in the direction she wanted them to go. Sometimes, coming
down the lane, the cows wandered from side to side, or escaped
into the wrong field. Mémé would call out shrilly in exasperation,
her voice would go up into a scream, she'd take it personally, whatever the cows were doing wrong this time, and she'd whack them
with her hazel twig. They didn't seem to mind. They lurched and
gambolled along.

In the morning I had my breakfast with Pépé in the kitchen.
Because he'd been so ill, he couldn't go out to work in the fields.
He had to rest. He might have to retire, my father had said to my
mother when they didn't know I was listening: and give up the
farm. Move nearer to us so we could keep an eye on both of
them.

I could hear Mémé dashing about outside seeing to the animals.
There was a great flapping and squawking of poultry, the dog was
barking, the cocks were crowing. Pépé and I sat at the table and
dunked bread and butter into our *café au lait*. Pépé sucked at his
very noisily, slurping it through his moustache. He was allowed to

sound so rude because he was the head of the family, and so old. His moustache was like a badge of this: very thick, and silky, and dark. When he kissed you the moustache was as soft as the brush he used for putting on his shaving soap. He didn't like beards and shaved his chin every day. The young men of his day, he explained to me, were proud of their fine moustaches. His worked like a sieve to strain his soup and his coffee, and, now, his soggy bread and butter. He liked making rude noises when he ate, and cracking jokes, and teasing Mémé. He called her the boss. She was the boss inside the house and he was outside. Only this morning his eyes were not sparkling, and he was thinner, and his hand shook, lifting the bread to his mouth.

We each had our favourite bowls, mine with the red stripe round the rim and his with the blue. He'd almost finished the coffee in his. Now, Mémé had instructed me, he was to sit by the fire and have a look at the newspaper. I was to do the washing-up.

– Pépé, I said to him: what would you do if you met the devil?

– Throw a bucket of cold water over him of course, Pépé said: he likes the heat, that one, cold water'd soon scare him off.

He was moving his chair back from the table. He put his fists on the table top and concentrated on starting to get up.

– Pépé, I said: can we still have the Easter egg hunt on Sunday? Like we always do?

It was hard for him to stand up. His legs wouldn't obey him, though he concentrated. His elbows shook, and his knees. Then he managed it. He gasped a bit, with his chin down, then he raised his head and grimaced at me.

– Yes of course we will, he said: you bet.

I hovered alongside while he tottered across the floor, using the back of a chair to support himself, then subsided on to the chair where Mémé and I had sat the night before. He didn't notice I was there, he was breathing with a whistling sound, sharp as the owls' call.

That was on Maundy Thursday. On Good Friday Pépé couldn't get out of bed. Something had hit him round the brain in the night and put him to sleep so he couldn't move or speak. He wouldn't be able to do any of his usual things: come out to pick primroses and violets and see how the animals and fields were getting along. It was the same illness as before, but worse this time. Mémé's face went loose and puffy with crying. She looked old. The ambulance arrived and took Pépé away to the hospital. His feet stuck out of the end of the stretcher.

All the family arrived to stay, to help Mémé, to look after the farm, to take turns visiting Pépé. Mémé wouldn't let me go to the hospital. She said it would upset me too much and I was too young. I heard her telling my mother. Pépé had tubes up his nose and into his arm and she didn't want me to be frightened. He didn't know anyone, she thought, even when they held his hand and spoke to him.

On the morning of Easter Sunday they all went to Mass, leaving me with my baby brother. I said I had a stomach-ache and a headache, I begged to stay behind.

I decided not to murder my baby brother just yet. I reasoned they'd know it was me, if they came home from church and found him dead with only me in the house. It was better to wait. Instead of murdering him I filled a bucket with cold water and emptied it out of my bedroom window, and then I went out into the garden, carrying my sleeping brother in his basket. I put him down on the grass, underneath the lilac bush at the edge of the vegetable garden. Now that I knew how to get rid of the devil, my baby brother would be safe. No harm could come to him, with the dog around to guard us both.

Pépé was at the far end of the vegetable plot, bending over a row of leeks with Mémé's shopping bag in one hand and something round and shining in the other. It was an Easter egg. He placed it under the thick, flopping leek, and straightened up. He took another egg out of his bag, wrapped in metallic paper that glinted green and blue in the sunlight. He stooped, and placed it in the curly leaves of a cabbage. Then he looked my way, and spotted me watching him. I saw his face move in a smile. He placed his forefinger against his moustache. A secret. The first time ever I'd actually caught him hiding my Easter eggs. It was supposed to be a mystery. I wasn't supposed to know.

The dog began to bark. The car ground into the yard. They were back from Mass already. Inside the house the telephone was ringing.

Pépé smiled at me very sweetly. He was too far away for me to touch him, but his gaiety and warmth crossed the garden, as certain as the Easter egg, wrapped in gold and silver paper, I cradled later that morning in my hands.

A BODICE RIPS

A NOVEL IN SEVEN CHAPTERS

for Sarah Le Fanu

CHAPTER ONE THE DIAMOND

There was no time to lose. Maria paused in the middle of the green and gold drawing-room, biting her lips and looking wildly around. At the same time she was listening for sounds from outside. She ran to one of the long windows and peered out, then ran back. Her movements were clumsy, as though she were not used to moving hurriedly, as though panic had robbed her of her normal grace acquired two years before at finishing school. She caught up her long dress of yellow satin in one hand, but even so it kept getting in the way.

At any moment Count Ferdinand would be here. Those who had experienced his justice called him Ferdinand the Terrible. His victims could expect no mercy. He was famous throughout Valsarnia and beyond for his ruthlessness. Even the Emperor, that feeble and ill old man who had appointed him Regent until the young heir should come of age, was in awe of Ferdinand.

Maria moved back towards the uncurtained window, to watch for the lights of a car gliding up the long hill through the blackness of the forest. She wondered what she should do.

Her fingers closed over the treasures in her palm that she had snatched up from her dressing-table and brought downstairs with her. A small wrought-iron key, dangling from a slender silver chain, and a diamond ring. She unclenched her fingers and glanced at the ring. She remembered Sylvester's expression as he had put the hoop of glittering stones into her hand half an hour earlier.

– This was my mother's, he had murmured: and now I am giving it to you.

Maria's heart had missed a beat, then started thumping. For a moment she thought he was about to ask her to marry him. But then she came back to reality. Sylvester was leader of the rebels. His life was vowed to serving the cause. He had often told her he could never marry. A wife was a luxury and would get in the way. He needed to be free, not to be tied down. To be able to depart at any moment, wherever the needs of the struggle sped him next. Moved by his selflessness, Maria had blushed and felt ashamed of the desires she dared not name. She had accepted the diamond ring and had promised to sell it for him as he wished and get the money to him via one of his comrades.

The circle of jewels on her open palm winked in the candlelight and the firelight. Somehow it seemed to be a symbol of strength. She breathed deeply, gathered herself to stillness, a semblance of calm, and took the only possible decision. She flung the silver chain over her head, dropping the small black key out of sight below the *décolletage* of her evening dress, and thrust the diamond ring into the pocket of her petticoat.

The long beams of two powerful headlights swept across the window. Tyres crunched over gravel. Car doors slammed. Men's voices rang out in the courtyard. The dogs barked. The bell clanged at the main entrance. Count Ferdinand the Terrible had arrived.

Maria clasped her hands together and turned resolutely to face the drawing-room door as though it were a firing-squad.

CHAPTER TWO CHILDHOOD

Maria was an orphan. Her mother had died giving birth to her and her father had been too griefstruck to marry again, preferring, instead, to dedicate himself to his beloved only child. She rarely saw him, because he threw himself into his work. He was a corset manufacturer who made his fortune when he patented his new invention and sold it to all the women of Valsarnia. The Revolutionary Bust and Stomach Stiffener, known to its devotees as the Squeasy, used thin ribs of steel to replace the strips of whalebone previously employed in ladies' foundation garments. The steel wands were inserted both horizontally and vertically, to provide a lattice of total control. Another distinctive feature of this flesh-hugging machine was that it was covered not with the usual pink linen or buckram but in canvas of the chastest and severest white. Maria's father died a happy man, on his daughter's eighteenth birthday, and left her a wardrobe full of corsets, a factory and a warehouse full of more corsets, and a corset business to run.

CHAPTER THREE　THE FUNERAL

Maria's father was buried in the regimental chapel of the great church in town. He had worshipped there every week for all of his adult life. Sunday after Sunday, while the padre intoned his sermon and exhorted his congregation to become soldiers of God, Maria's father had gazed dreamily at the regimental banners hung along the nave, the marble monuments to valiant generals slain on the parade-grounds in time of violence and upheaval, the crossed swords and bayonets that decorated the columns, and the tall stained-glass windows behind the high altar that depicted the heroic knights of the holy tradition: St Michael the Archangel, the devil-slayer, St George, the dragon-slayer, and the patron saint of Valsarnia, St Victor, the serpent-slayer. Completely covered from head to toe in heavy silvery armour they raised their mailed fists and waved their huge spears aloft. Under their spurred and booted feet they trampled the writhing and wriggling symbols of evil, the wily and scaly snake-monsters with lascivious faces. The saints' helmets were wreathed with the lilies of purity. Their visors were pulled down.

It was here, one drowsy Sunday morning, that Maria's father had received the first glimmerings of his great idea. He went home for Sunday lunch, his imagination filled with images of stern goodness encased in armour-plating, and gave his daughter his customary Sunday kiss. She wriggled and squirmed, laughing, in his arms. Her softness filled him with unease, with a kind of distaste. The idea of the Revolutionary Bust and Stomach Stiffener was born.

Now his sable-draped coffin stood on a bier surrounded by tall candles. The regimental choir sang the martial hymns Maria's father had so loved. The old padre spoke of the battle of the soul, of the valour and cleanness and uprightness of the true knight of God. The mourners, mainly old soldiers, stared at Maria, so young and so beautiful, her face peeping out of her black fur-lined hood, her hands hidden in her black fur muff, her little feet encased in high-heeled black ankle boots.

Leaving the churchyard, Maria dropped a long black suede glove. Her tightly laced corset did not allow her to bend and pick it up. Sylvester, who had been lounging elegantly under the yew trees at the gate, on the lookout for possible recruits to the cause, picked up the glove, kissed it and returned it to her. Thus they became acquainted.

– How shall I ever live up to my father's memory? Maria asked Sylvester in desperation one day soon afterwards: when I feel so weak and powerless and alone?

Sylvester replied: You can support those fighting for a just cause, for an end to tyranny, for the overthrow of despotism!

Maria was fired up in a moment by his valour. She was converted rapidly to the rebels' cause. Sylvester swore her to secrecy, and they pricked their thumbs and mixed their blood as a symbol of their pact. The Confederates, as the band of revolutionaries was called, needed money, a safe haven. Maria delightedly supplied both, emptying her bank account and making her new friends free of her house. She promised Sylvester, on pain of death, that she would never betray him and his comrades to the terrible Count Ferdinand, who was Commander-in-Chief of the army as well as Regent of the Kingdom, and who was known to throw his enemies into windowless underground cells for life, if, indeed, he did not simply have them beheaded in the city square. Maria was happy. Women could not, of course, be Confederates, but she was the next best thing. She was a Confederate's girlfriend. She was in love with Sylvester.

Her love made her so bold that she dared to offer him more than money, more than a hiding-place. She bent over him, one day, as he studied possible escape routes on the map spread out on the table in her dining-room, and murmured: Take me, Sylvester! Take me!

Absorbed in his plans, he did not hear her whispered entreaty. She repeated her words more loudly. Sylvester sighed and looked up.

– Not now, darling, he reproached her: not just before the start of a campaign! I must save all my energies for the struggle!

He glanced at the clock on the mantelpiece.

– It's your turn to keep watch. Off you go.

Maria climbed the stairs to her room. She would have liked to run, but her heavy steel-lined corset made free movement impossible. Blinking back her tears, she stood on guard by the casement, upright as one of the Imperial sentries, vigilant as one of the saintly knights in silvery armour depicted on the stained-glass windows of the regimental chapel. She peered through the uncurtained pane into the gathering dusk. Nothing stirred.

The telephone rang. Maria walked across to her little writing-table and picked up the receiver.

It was a woman's voice that spoke, deep and contralto.

– Tell Sylvester to fly. Count Ferdinand has been tipped off as to his whereabouts and is moving in through the forest. He is bound to search your house. Tell Sylvester to hurry. Tell him I shall be waiting for him on the seashore, with the boat.

The voice was urgent, harsh. The woman rang off abruptly. Maria put the phone down. Then she picked it up again. The line had gone dead.

Maria opened her bedroom door with trembling hands. She clutched the banister of the staircase to steady herself. She had not expected discovery so soon. Something had gone wrong. Danger was very close. Count Ferdinand, she was certain, from what the voice on the phone had said, had been alerted to her part in the plot. She shuddered at the thought of him entering her house and questioning her. But if only she could get Sylvester away to safety, she knew that she could brave anything for his sake. She lifted her chin and walked downstairs very slowly, unable to hurry because of the tight lacing of her steel-lined stays.

In the green and gold drawing-room she told Sylvester about the phone message and showed him the entrance, hidden behind a panel of the wainscoting, to the secret passage which led out into the cave in the forest. A woodcutter, who was an ally of the Confederates, lived nearby, and would be at the ready for anyone

issuing from the cave and giving the password. The password was
Sylvester's code name: Far-Off.

Sylvester pressed his mother's diamond ring into Maria's hands,
urging her to sell it for as much as possible and to send the money
on to him via the woodcutter. Carla would do the rest.

– That wonderful Carla, he exclaimed: she's never let me down
yet.

– Who's Carla? Maria asked.

But there was no time to waste in idle chatter. There was no
time for tearful farewells, for fond embraces. Sylvester dived into
the secret passage, and Maria locked the door after him and closed
the concealing panel. She carried the key and the diamond ring
out of the room with her, biting her lip.

She went slowly back up the stairs. The main thing was to
stand firm, to keep the faith. She must fight the good fight, act
normally, and pretend to be greatly surprised that anyone should
accuse her of being mixed up in revolutionary politics.

First of all, therefore, she decided to change into evening dress,
as she usually did at dinner-time. Her father had always liked her
to dress for dinner and she had not yet broken herself of the habit.
Besides she had so many evening frocks it was a pity not to wear
them. Accordingly, she rang for her maid and asked her to unlace
her corset, which did up at the back with a steel string and fifty
little steel hooks.

The maid struggled and panted. At last the steel cage was off. It
fell, clanging, on to the floor. Maria's flesh leaped out.

She bathed hurriedly. Then it was time to put the corset back
on. Now Maria's unflinching loyalty to her father suddenly

wavered. She foresaw an evening of possible physical activity, in which she might be required to run up and down stairs several times, sending semaphore messages from windows or checking the telephone in her bedroom, or leading Count Ferdinand on a wild-goose chase away from the door to the secret passage. She would need to be able to move fast, as Sylvester did. Therefore she would not be able to wear her corset. She bent her head in anguish.

– Forgive me, Father! she cried.

She threw the corset into the corner of the room. It seemed to her that all the warrior saints in the regimental chapel hung their heads in shame. She had abandoned their high ideals. She had betrayed their beautiful code of chivalry.

– Forgive me, Father! she moaned again.

Then she selected her favourite evening dress from the wardrobe and slipped it on. It buttoned up at the front, the little cloth-covered buttons concealed under a fold of material. Rather than steel cutting into her through canvas, she now had the delicious sensation of thick, rich satin next to her skin, flowing over her soft flesh as smooth and cool as milk. She lifted the yellow folds in her hands and stroked them. Her petticoat was the merest wisp of gossamer swishing against her thighs. She put on her best amber and pearl tiara, hooked topaz rings into her ears, clasped on a few gold bracelets, picked up the diamond ring and the key from her dressing-table, and stepped into her gold evening slippers.

Then she ran downstairs.

It was such a marvellous experience that she ran back up and then ran down again. And then up again and then down again.

Then she stood in the drawing-room, her bosom heaving. She

was panting and flushed. Her eyes sparkled with the unwonted exercise. Her mind raced. She was frightened for Sylvester, and determined to save him from the clutches of Count Ferdinand, but she was also preoccupied and puzzled by the mysterious woman's voice on the telephone. Who could she be? Did Sylvester have *two* benefactresses? Maria clasped her hands together in anguish. But it was too late for thoughts of jealousy. Ferdinand was in her house. Any moment he would be in the room, confronting her. She had the key and the diamond ring safely hidden on her person. All she had to do now was play her part. Stall him as long as possible. Give Sylvester time to get away.

Standing as erect as possible on the soft carpet of her drawing-room, listening to the firm, determined tread of the man ascending the stairs outside, she felt her cheeks flame and her mind whirl with images. The diamond ring and the key hidden inside her dress . . . Sylvester creeping out of the secret tunnel into the cave . . . her father's coffin draped in black . . . the warrior saints with their stern mouths . . . the woodcutter waiting in the dark forest outside the entrance to the cave.

She lifted her chin and trembled with fear. The door swung open and he strode in.

So *this*, Maria thought: was Count Ferdinand the Terrible.

CHAPTER FOUR   FERDINAND THE TERRIBLE

Authority emanated from him like a physical force. Maria knew she must not respond, must not give way. Yet her body suddenly felt pliant, as though simply by entering the room he had over-powered her. She forced herself to look at him steadily.

He was a tall, commanding figure dressed in the uniform of his élite crack corps of horsemen, the Dark Riders. He wore a black tunic, black breeches, and highly polished black riding boots. A long black cloak swept back over one shoulder and was fastened at the front with gold clasps in the form of lions. Gold braid edged his epaulettes and cuffs. A single gold stud shone on his high black collar. He carried leather riding gloves, a black cap with a gold plume, in one hand, and a riding-crop in the other.

His dark face, with its deep-set black eyes and ironic mouth under a thin line of black moustache, was stern. He bowed to her and clicked his heels, and she felt sure he was mocking her.

– You know what I've come for, he said: Far-Off Sylvester. Where is he?

Maria gasped. If indeed he knew Sylvester's secret code name, the game was certainly up. She could hear the tramp of feet all over the house, as the Dark Riders searched high and low for the leader of the rebels. Play for time, she thought. This was not difficult. She found that she could not speak, so transfixed was she by terror.

She was face to face, after so long, with the most feared man in the kingdom, he who was spoken of only in whispers, he who had the ear of the dying Emperor and was acting Regent until the Emperor's young son should be of age to rule. Folk said that Ferdinand would never give up his power. Under cover of crushing the rebellion led by Sylvester, he would establish his dominion ever more firmly and force the rightful heir to give up all claim to the throne. Looking at Ferdinand's haughty face, Maria could well believe it. Her voice, when at last she found it, was hoarse.

– Go away, Count. You are mistaken in your suspicions. I know nothing of anyone called Sylvester.

Ferdinand smiled at her grimly.

– You are a brave woman, but also a foolish one. We followed Sylvester all the way to your house, we saw him come in, and we know from your housekeeper, who opened the door to us just now, that there is a secret passage leading out of your drawing-room, to whose door you alone have the key. Your housekeeper, I fear, is not above a bribe.

He showed his teeth in a sardonic smile as he watched Maria turn white.

– Don't lie to me, he said: and don't try to play games with me. Else I shall be provoked into playing them with you.

Maria's armpits were wet with sweat. She forced herself to look straight back at him.

– What kind of games, Count?

The dark eyes, with something unfathomable as well as ironic in their depths, were fixed on hers. He put down his leather riding gloves, his riding-crop, and his plumed cap on the side table against the wall by the door, and advanced towards her where she stood in the centre of the room. His movements were swift and decided. He had the bearing and gestures of a man habituated to command. His face was hard, but the mobile mouth relaxed as he looked at her.

Maria flinched as he approached, but she held her ground. She shivered suddenly, wishing she had thrown a stole over her arms and breast, for she was naked above the low-cut gold satin frock except for a band of gold tulle that encircled her shoulders. Her full long skirt swung out in a soft bell. She plunged her hands through the invisible slits cut in the sides of her gown, into the pockets of her petticoat. Her left hand touched the diamond ring hidden there. She looked at Ferdinand as haughtily as possible. Now that he was so close to her she could see the softness of his black eyelashes, of his close-cropped black hair. She could see that his thin, fine face was a little careworn. His features were clear-cut. His mouth looked as though it could be cruel.

CHAPTER FIVE A GAME OF HIDE AND SEEK

Ferdinand moved forward again. Maria's right hand flew out of her pocket and leaped to the silver chain which showed its glint at her neck and fell into the bosom of her gown. She took a step backwards. Ferdinand followed.

– Just give me the key to the door of the secret passage, he said: there's no need to be afraid of me. I shan't hurt you.

– I'm not afraid of you, Maria said, hating her trembling voice: even though your behaviour is outrageous, forcing your way in here like this.

His lips twisted.

– That is something, at least. I'm glad you are not afraid of me. As for forcing my way in, I am on the Emperor's business and I have the Emperor's signature on a search warrant to go through your house until I find the traitor Sylvester whom you are hiding.

I should warn you that unless you co-operate with me I shall have you searched too. Now give me that key.

He reached out and put his hands on her arms. She jerked with shock. Her eyes flew to his. He moved his hands slowly and deliberately up her bare forearms, over her elbows, to her shoulders, grasping the swathe of gold tulle that encircled them. She kept very still under his touch. She felt the warmth of the contact, ten little points of fire burning through the tulle, two patches of fire that were his palms. He gripped her shoulders harder. His face was close to hers. The dark, intent face of a stranger who was treating her as though he knew her intimately, who had dared to take her by the arms and slide his hands slowly up to her shoulders in a threatening caress.

His voice was quiet.

– Your gestures have told me where you have hidden the key. If you won't give it to me freely, of your own accord, I shall have to take it. Do you understand?

A wave of fear mixed with excitement rushed over her. She felt her face washed by blushes of red. She managed to speak.

– I don't know what you mean. I haven't got the key.

He shrugged. His hands moved to the front of her dress. He studied the concealing fold of satin that covered the bodice, then slid his fingers underneath it and found the little buttons. Taking his time, leisurely and deliberate in his movements, he began unbuttoning Maria's dress. One button slipped out of its buttonhole, then another. The top of the dress parted, began to gape open. Ferdinand's hands moved further down, closed around the third button, the fourth. They were little satin-covered knobs, of the same yellow as the dress. They opened easily; they fell under his thumb and slid out of their yellow holes. The dress was so designed that you could put it on and take it off yourself, quickly, without needing to call for someone to come and help you get in and out of it, to fasten and unfasten it at the back. Maria had chosen this dress precisely because it was not like a corset. To wear it she did not have to depend on anyone else.

Maria stood proud and still, with the air of an unwilling captive. Ferdinand was standing so close to her that she could see every line and flourish of the rampant gold lions engraved on the clasps of his black cloak. At the first touch of his fingers on her skin she had felt that she would faint. The shock of the touch brought with it a pleasure over which she had no control. His fingers went on making contact with her flesh. Cool and sure, they inserted themselves between cloth and her body. He was opening the panels of satin very slowly, letting the dress reveal her nakedness. The dress being unloosed, expertly parted inch by satin inch, allowed the warmth of the candles and the fire in the grate to move over her. She felt she glowed golden like them. Her heart pounded. She could smell something hot and sweet, like the crushed petals of flowers.

The fingers working on the buttons, grazing her with caresses as they went, moving in and out between the dress and her skin, reached her waist at last. Maria breathed deeply. She shuddered as a wave of sweetness pushed through her. She tried to keep still but she was trembling. She needed to sit down.

Ferdinand paused. His face was faintly amused. Maria stared back at him. He lifted his hands and tugged at the two sides of the dress, pulling it off her shoulders so that it fell down around her waist, in crumpled gold satin folds.

She could not speak. He lifted the key, which was slung on the thin silver chain that dangled from round her neck to lie in the curved hollow between her breasts. The clasp of the chain had worked its way round to lie next to the key. Ferdinand lifted it away from her skin, using both hands, and opened it. He pulled the chain away from her neck, off her, and put chain and key into his breeches pocket.

CHAPTER SIX THE HUNT GOES ON

Ferdinand lifted the fallen folds of the bodice of Maria's dress, pulled them up, covered her shoulders once more. He rebuttoned the yellow satin into place. He did it efficiently and swiftly, like a mother getting a child ready for school. Maria stood obediently in front of him. She ached and burned at each light, deft touch, as his fingers strayed across the slippery material covering her skin. Far too thin, the cloth, which clung then slid, as he made it move on her flesh, and she could not stop herself from shuddering with pleasure.

She could not look at him. He fastened the top button. He took her hand and lifted it. She felt his lips touch it. She snatched it back as though he'd bitten her. His voice was gentle.

– Thank you. You made my task far less unpleasant than it might have been, and I am very grateful.

Maria watched him turn, go straight to the secret panel in the wainscoting, swing it open, unlock the door behind, and pull this open in turn. She thought: He knew where it was all along. How? And then she remembered the housekeeper, who had given in so easily to a bribe, and told all she knew.

– Sylvester is long gone, isn't he? Ferdinand said: he'll be at the other end by now, coming out into the cave. My men will be waiting for him there. We've got the woodcutter and we'll get Sylvester.

He frowned.

– Nevertheless, we'll search the tunnel. Just to make sure. And you and I will wait here, while the search is carried out.

He shouted, and two Dark Riders came running. They stooped, and entered the little door into the secret passage. It swallowed them up and they were gone.

Maria forced herself to raise her eyes and look at Ferdinand. His gaze was whimsical. He strolled back across the room and halted in front of her. Her lips buzzed and stung. Her knees felt weak and shook.

Ferdinand's tone was conversational and bland.

– And the diamond ring left to me by my mother that Sylvester stole from me? Where have you hidden that, may I ask? Are you going to tell me, or are you going to force me to look for that too?

Maria jumped. But before she could move a step his hands shot out and caught her. His breath was hot in her ear.

– Oh yes, Sylvester is my brother. Didn't you know? He wants to be Regent, and who can blame him? Unfortunately, it is I whom the Emperor has chosen, being the elder, to guard the interests of his heir, and see that he comes into his kingdom when the time arrives.

– You're lying, Maria panted: I don't believe you.

Struggling to get away, she caught her high-heeled shoe in a fold of her dress and tripped. He pulled her further off balance, so that she toppled into his arms, which closed around her and held her up. Once more his hands pushed her dress off her shoulders, but this time roughly. Holding her in a vice-like grip with one arm, he caressed her neck and shoulders, tugging down the swathe of tulle, while she tried uselessly to fight him and he laughed. His caresses were tender as silk. His hand ripped open the front of her dress, no wasting time on buttons, and stroked her breast, pinching the nipple gently until a moan escaped from Maria's lips. Then he pushed Maria's chin up, forcing her mouth against his, making her lips yield and open. She shook against him. Her insides churned. She tore her mouth away from his.

– No, she whispered: no, I haven't got the diamond ring. I don't know what you're talking about.

He lifted his head and looked at her. His eyes glittered, black and sardonic. His voice was harsh.

– Let us stop fencing. You have fought well but your fight is over. Sylvester was captured in the forest by my men, before I entered this house. We've got Carla too.

He paused. Maria was shivering. The very air between them seemed to quiver with menace. She felt dazed. Perhaps, she thought confusedly, this was what hunted animals experienced when cornered, face to face with the huntsman at last. The game was up.

He tightened his grip on her. She disdained to struggle and to give him the pleasure of knowing how easily he could overpower her. She lowered her eyes and bit her lip.

Ferdinand was regarding her grimly.

– I'm afraid your friends are less faithful than you, he said: the woodcutter betrayed you, just as your housekeeper did, and just as Sylvester did. Once he realized he was fairly caught he did not scruple to give me the name I wanted. Offered the choice between life imprisonment and exile, Far-Off chose exile. And as part of the bargain he named his second most important accomplice after Carla. You. You've supplied him with money and sanctuary, but all this time, I'm afraid, he's been using you. He has abandoned you without a care for your safety.

Maria heard these words in silence. It was the end. It was all over. Sometime, the shock and numbness would wear off and she would feel . . . what? Sylvester had not been loyal to her. She had merely been his tool. He had cast her aside in order to save his own skin. Later on she would find out what she felt. At the moment she was aware only of being held in Ferdinand's powerful embrace, of his dark face close to hers.

She had the oddest sense that she had known all along that Sylvester was not to be trusted. That woman on the telephone. Carla. Of course, she must have been his lover all the time.

– But he's your brother, she exclaimed faintly: how can you send him into exile?

– Better exile than life imprisonment or death, Ferdinand said: just as it was better to capture him in the forest than here, and so implicate you. I wished to spare you.

– Why should you be generous to me? she whispered: when I have fought and resisted you at every turn, when I believed all the lies Sylvester told me about you?

His mocking smile was back.

– Perhaps because I wish to get back the diamond ring and keep it for myself, before I decide whom to give it to.

He moved rapidly, without warning. Still gripping her, he bent forwards and sideways. His hand picked up her skirts in bunched folds, plunged beneath them. Startled, Maria cried out. She felt his mouth gently bite her earlobe, before his voice spoke hotly into her ear.

– You've got it in a pocket somewhere. And I'm going to search you until I find it.

His hand scooped up layers of dress and petticoat, inserted itself between dress and skin. Maria twisted in his grip, her legs pressed tightly together, then forced apart by his fingers which relentlessly explored between her knees and up, further up, while he supported her with one arm around her back, making her lean away from him while his hand dived repeatedly into her skirts, and she clutched and thrust at him and cried out, ohhhh, as he parted the lips of her pocket and was in, there, home, holding and stroking her diamond ring gently, repeatedly, endlessly, firmly, while she clenched her teeth trying not to cry out again but not able to stop herself: ohhhh. Life was certainly dangerous when you did not wear a corset. You were certainly not safe. You were not in control.

CHAPTER SEVEN THE KEY

The game was loosely based on the plot of *The Black Riders* by Violet Needham, which Maria had got out of the local children's library. She made up her own version of the story, which she preferred to the one in the book. She felt that hers was more true, that it contained all the bits underneath and in between, which Violet Needham did not spell out because she was writing for children, after all, who were not supposed to imagine such things.

Sometimes Maria played the heroine's role, and sometimes her cousin Nanda did. Whoever was the man had to be both Sylvester and Ferdinand, one after the other, and it did require a certain acting ability, to be capable of becoming both the perfidious villain and the dashing hero, and indeed to convey which was which. Maria was better at playing the man than Nanda was, but on the other hand she loved being the woman, and feeling all that delicious fear. Sometimes she thought it would be easier if she acted all by herself and played both parts, and lying in bed at night she could do this. But there was no denying the pleasure to be gained from doing it with someone else, especially someone like Nanda whom Maria could order around and who did what she was told, cracking her whip and stroking her moustache before ripping open Maria's dress.

They were ten at the time, and took their games seriously. They rehearsed over and over, even though nobody would ever see the performance but themselves. The rehearsals were the best part, especially at the end, because they never let themselves get there. They went over and over it, the moment when Ferdinand caresses

Maria so powerfully, and they knew that was the best moment, the one just before the end, when you can imagine the moment will never cease, that this exquisite painful explosive need will go on rising up and up like a rocket, they will remain in that state of heightened tension desiring each other madly with all their future ahead of them, a moment that doesn't have to end, a game that never has to be over because it can be repeated for ever. The game would always be there, and this present tense. It could be repeatedly rerun, like the ciné film of their childhood. Maria was a child pornographer; shamelessly she corrupted her cousin Nanda and got her to join in.

THE MIRACLE

Bella was tall and fair and commandingly good-looking. She wore a black beret and a tightly belted olive trenchcoat like a Resistance heroine in a Hollywood movie. She didn't smile at me when Saul introduced us. She pursed her scarlet lips while her blue eyes swivelled about. She commiserated wordlessly with Saul, in sidelong looks, on the smallness and remoteness of my house, the mud and cowpats in the lane, the overgrown garden which I thought so wild and romantic but which, when I looked at it now, was simply full of weeds. I showed her the guestroom, the bathroom and lavatory, and watched her eyebrows twitch up. I suppose my living arrangements were rather primitive but to me they were quaint, with a certain charm. It's all a matter of taste. We obviously read different style magazines.

Bella began talking to Saul about the house in the Lot-et-Garonne in which she had spent her summer holiday last year, its carefully distressed pink walls, its fabulous swimming-pool, its eighteenth-century furniture, its dovecote and vineyard and wisteria-hung terraces. I interrupted her and suggested a drink.

On Saturday morning we went to the local market to buy bread for lunch, which we ate indoors as it was raining. I laid the table with a clean white cloth and my best plates, set out our hors d'oeuvres of pâté and gherkins, olives, and celeriac *en rémoulade*. Then Saul and I ate *moules à la marinière*. Bella rejected this food, since she had just been diagnosed with a dairy and wheat allergy and kept to a low-fat diet and was convinced that shellfish didn't agree with her. She ate the rice cakes she had brought with her instead. I shouldn't have minded but I did, I felt frustrated and cross for reasons which I knew were to do with maternal and feminine wishes to give, and Bella denying me that pleasure, also not allowing me any power over her. Feeding herself, she remained independent, less of a guest. Her calm refusal of my food made me feel less mistress of my own house.

Analysing all this did not make me any the less childishly resentful. As a result I drank too much wine and got tiddly and talked too much. Showing off, Bella's expression called it. I slunk off to my room with a headache and fell into bed.

Later on in the afternoon, as it was still too wet to go for a walk or sit outside, we went back into town to have a look at the church. This was a large, airy, gothic structure, which was always empty. You could stroll about admiring the rose windows and the various medieval statues of the Virgin dotted around without worrying that you might be disturbing someone's prayers. I showed Saul and Bella the curtained-off little chapel behind the main altar with its miraculous silver-coated statue of Our Lady of the Thorn, surrounded by ex-votos and racks of candles alight with quivering pale flames.

Saul had seen this dark little interior before, of course, but he enthused over the faded fourteenth-century frescoes and the worn seventeenth-century tapestries on the walls as though he were a first-time visitor. Saul had a kind nature, which was one reason why I loved him. He wanted the people he loved to get on with each other, he tried to make his friends happy, and so he cheerfully tolerated me as I pointed out the plaster statue of St Antony, nineteenth-century admittedly but nonetheless charming, which perched on a side table near the holy water stoup, with a bunch of snowy lilies in a blue plastic vase nearby and a little votive light winking in a red glass dish.

– He's the best saint of all, I said: he performs miracles. He finds things when you've lost them.

I could hear the *faux-naïf* tone of my voice but couldn't alter it. Cutesy-pie, gushy and silly. I loathed myself. Perhaps because I could see that Bella, so sophisticated in her knee-length black leather coat and fur-trimmed velvet gauntlets, was bored with me and the rain and the church and the weekend visit that was not turning out well, I babbled on. I explained how years ago I had been to St Antony's shrine in Padua, gaudily decorated in elaborate versions of the baroque, and brought back a statue of him that changed colour according to the weather, how the public lavatories just outside his basilica were labelled Cabinets of Decency, and how I had learned to address the saint in Italian, a special prayer that was a rhyming couplet so that you could easily remember it.

Bella turned away and thrust her arm through Saul's. She obviously disapproved of visiting anything in Padua quite so kitsch. The famous Giotto frescoes should be enough for anyone. Anyone with proper art historical taste that is.

– It's horribly damp in here, darling, she said: and freezing cold. Do let's go and get a drink.

We left the church and settled in the café outside. Rain swept in gusts against the steamed-up windows. We huddled in our coats on chilly metal chairs and rubbed our hands together.

– We need warming up, Saul said: let's order some cognac.

Bella's cheeks went pink as she tossed back her amber glassful. She took off her gloves, reapplied scarlet lipstick and frowned into the mirror of her compact.

– The trouble with you, she suddenly said to me: is that you're not a proper ex-Catholic. You haven't thought it right through and become a real atheist. You still think all this folklore is so appealing. It's a form of slumming really, the way you carry on. You ignore the authoritarianism of the Church and just pick out the pretty bits. You're just a spiritual tourist. Still believing in miracles in this day and age. It's ridiculous.

This was perhaps the second time since she had arrived at my house the evening before that Bella had bothered to address me so I felt I should look grateful. I felt myself glaring. She went on to explain in a loud, firm voice that miracles were simply a figure of speech. People used the word loosely and lazily to denote anything they did not understand and whose workings they held in awe. Man-made technology had replaced the power of God but superstitious and ignorant people treated it with the same reverence they

previously accorded to their imaginary deity and invested it with
the same old magical capacity.

– Television would have seemed like a miracle to you at one
time, she pointed out: if you'd lived all your life in a place that
didn't have it, and then you suddenly saw it. A bit like how
you feel about computers these days, perhaps. I noticed when
you showed us round that yours is the most basic word-
processor you can buy. You can't even e-mail people. You can't
access the Net. And you were telling Saul over lunch how you
still like to write certain letters by hand. You haven't got a television either, have you? Machines are obviously an aspect of
contemporary culture that baffles you so you regard them with
exaggerated deference. But they're only tools. They're for us to
make use of, not to be enslaved by.

I signalled to the waiter for more cognac. The aspect of contemporary culture that I found more baffling than computers was
Saul's choice of new lover. How could he like someone who was so
sharp and snooty? Perhaps he didn't like her, though, but liked sex
with her. Perhaps she wasn't so snooty in bed, once she'd taken off
her black beret and gauntlets. Or perhaps she wore them even in
bed and that was what turned Saul on: a woman naked except for
her hat and gloves. I'd have stripped and dressed like that for Saul.
But he'd never fancied me. It struck me that I was simply a jealous
possessive monster who couldn't bear to see Saul happy with
anyone else but myself. What a bitch I was. I felt depressed.

Saul was leaning back in his chair, smiling, relieved that at least
Bella and I were talking to each other. He'd been so sure we would
hit it off. We both loved him, didn't we? He and I had known each

other since our student days, learned how to drink, dance and do drugs together, seen each other through love affairs, in and out of a marriage apiece. We were like brother and sister. For the last ten years we'd made a point of spending a week together every spring somewhere in Europe. It had become a cherished ritual. Last year, after being made redundant, I had left London and moved to the French countryside. Saul had been the first visitor to my tiny rented house. In between seeing each other we talked on the phone. We wrote letters. I kept a photo of him on my desk. I should have been glad he had fallen in love at last with someone who loved him back (did she – how could I tell?), but I was too mean. I missed our old routines, the conversations over the fire lasting late into the night, the long walks in the woods, the elaborate meals we cooked together. I told myself I'd feel less jealous if Bella had made the smallest effort to be nice to me. It was all her fault.

I could see that Bella did not care how I felt, because I didn't matter to her. I was not important. She had to put up with me on this visit because I was Saul's oldest woman friend and therefore we had to be introduced, but the only person who interested her was Saul. She would make sure, I thought, if she and Saul lasted as a couple, that he and I would see less of each other from now on, that the annual spring meetings would stop. Strange how much it hurt to be so snubbed, to be regarded with such indifference.

My vanity was wounded. I wasn't accustomed to thinking of myself as quite so boring. I had amusing stories to tell about my encounters with plumbers and roofers and electricians, tales that I'd been saving up to tell my next visitors, that I'd tweaked into shape over the long winter evenings spent staring at the fire. But even Saul indulged me less than usual. He kept referring to films and plays I hadn't seen, newspaper articles I hadn't read, concerts I hadn't been to. Then I could see him making a conscious effort to draw me into his conversation with Bella.

During that long, rainy weekend Bella provided me with excellent opportunities for self-mortification. In her company I necessarily practised humility and self-abasement. Had I remained a proper Catholic rather than the half-hearted ex Bella accused me of being, had I truly been striving for sainthood, I should have welcomed this occasion of crushing my self-esteem underfoot and so growing in holiness. As it was, I thought she was unfriendly, nasty, rude and bad-mannered, and I couldn't see at all why Saul fancied her and I couldn't wait for them to leave.

On Saturday night I carefully cooked a supper Bella could eat. Oven-roasted vegetables tossed in the minimum of olive oil, grilled mackerel with sorrel sauce minus the cream, plain brown rice, green salad with the dressing on the side, poached pears with no extra sugar. I drank too much wine again, got tiddly again, made an excuse and went to bed early, leaving them tucked up together on the sofa by the fire. I couldn't stand watching Bella lay her head on Saul's shoulder, giggle up at him, kiss him as though I weren't in the room, sitting opposite, forced to watch. I couldn't bear the way he beamingly accepted these caresses without noticing my angry embarrassment.

The rain stopped just as I was slipping into sleep. I heard it cease against my window-pane, replaced by a hush in which the owls hooted long and slow, that cool, melancholy call of the hunters, first in the woods behind the house and then close by. The front door opened with a creak, and I heard my guests laughing as they peered out into the garden.

Sunday morning shone, the world brilliant with sunlight refracting off raindrops. They hung, full and glittering, on every grass-blade, every leaf. They dangled so heavily that you marvelled they did not fall. We had breakfast sitting under the little glass porch that arched over the front steps. We bunched up close together, sheltered and warm, looking at the wet lavender bushes where light glanced and flashed on caught beads of water. Saul and I had coffee and croissants. Bella had rice cakes and camomile tea, a sachet taken from the selection she'd brought with her.

They were due to leave at midday, to drive to St Malo to catch the afternoon boat. At half past eleven, Bella, checking her bags, announced she had lost her passport.

We hunted through the house as purposefully as owls. No passport. Bella was adamant she had had it in her shoulder-bag when she arrived. She had noticed it on Friday evening when she first fished for her sachets of herb tea. But now it had vanished. We looked in all the improbable places as well as the likely ones, but it hadn't fallen down behind a sofa cushion or the lavatory or the fridge; it wasn't hiding in the breadbin or the egg basket or the bookcase. The house was so small we were able to search it several times in twenty minutes. No passport anywhere.

Bella was tense-faced. She wound a blonde curl round her middle finger and tugged on it.

– They'll never let me back in to the country without a passport. You know what they're like at Immigration. They'll never believe that I simply lost the wretched thing. But it'll take ages to apply for a new one – oh what shall I do?

I was so desperate for her to leave that I became inspired.

– We'll have to pray to St Antony, I announced: there's only one thing for it. We'll have to ask him to work a miracle and find it.

Bella assumed I was mocking her and glared at me. Saul looked exasperated with both of us.

– Come on, darling, he said: it's not the end of the world. We can ring up the consulate in Paris if necessary and ask them to help.

The thought of Bella having to stay on longer in my house while she applied for a new passport spurred me on. I raised my hands against my companions' impatient sighs.

– Shut up for a minute. Let me concentrate.

The couplet I had learned in Padua came back to me. I recited it in the loud, confident voice necessary for addressing a busy saint.

– SANT' ANTONIO DALLA BARBA BIANCA

FAI MI TROVARE COSA CHE MI MANCA.

We were all silent for a few moments before half-heartedly resuming our search. Saul lifted the corner of the rug to peer at the skin of dust on the floor underneath. Bella stretched up and ran her hand along the high stone lip of the mantelpiece. I inspected the heap of papers crouching under the telephone. None of us spoke.

In the hush, it became clear, a few minutes later, that a car was driving rapidly up the lane towards the house. It clattered to a stop in a grind of gravel just as I reached the front door and wrenched it open.

Out of a battered Renault 4 jumped a middle-aged woman I had never seen before, curly-haired, pink-faced and triumphantly smiling, wearing a pink flowered cotton frock and wellington boots. In her hand she waved Bella's passport.

We sat and had a cognac to celebrate. My newly met neighbour, Madame Melard, explained that her two workmen had been moving cows between pastures, going along the track in the woods behind the house, when they spotted the passport lying in the long grass at the edge of the path. Not knowing what it was, having admired the photograph of the *jolie nana*, they had been about to throw it into the nearby pond when something stopped them and they decided instead to take it back to the farm to show to their employer. Madame Melard, recognizing it as some kind of *pièce d'identité* in a foreign language, knowing that she had a new neighbour who was English, had put two and two together and dashed over, just in time to save the day.

– Oh I never thought, Bella said: of course we did go for a midnight walk in the woods, because the rain had stopped and we heard the owls and the moonlight was so beautiful. I took my shoulder-bag with me, of course, and the flap must have fallen open or something.

Madame Melard shook her head sternly at her.

– You must not do that again. This time, you were lucky.

I tried to repress a smug smile. How wonderful to hear someone telling Bella off.

– Thanks to St Antony, I said: it's all due to him. He worked us a miracle.

The effects of the saint's intervention did not stop here. St Antony had obviously decided I lacked a lot, so piled my lap with gifts. For a start, Madame Melard quickly became a good friend. She took me under her wing, taught me gardening and Breton cooking, supervised my attempts at fitting in to country life. With characteristic frankness she told me I wasn't much good at it. She said I was a real townie at heart. Why pretend otherwise?

Another aspect of the miracle was that Bella wrote to me. A handwritten letter. She thanked me for a fascinating weekend and also explained how much she had disliked me at first because she was so jealous; I was Saul's closest woman friend; I had seemed so standoffish and priggish and cold; I was so independent that she felt inadequate. I rang her up and thanked her in return.

We got into the habit of chatting regularly on the telephone. We discovered that, just as Saul had hoped and predicted, we got on well. We sparred, like girls in the playground. We knocked our rough bits together and smoothed our corners down.

Bella told me during one of these phone conversations that she had developed a new theory of miracles. She decided that miracles were really about people's love of story-telling, fitting odd bits of your life into a pattern that you invented yourself, stringing them together into a narrative, making a shape that pleased you. I expounded this idea to Madame Melard one afternoon, when I had finished helping her plant the peas in her vegetable patch and we were drinking coffee at her kitchen table.

Madame Melard paused and frowned. She shrugged. Then she began telling me about her wonderful new computer which did all her tax and VAT accounts in the twinkling of an eye, and let her send invoices by e-mail, and about her new portable phones which enabled her to stay in close contact with all her workmen out in the fields. Now that I'd acknowledged I was defeated in my attempts to live in the Breton countryside, she commented, and had decided to pack up and return to London, I would have to get myself a decent computer too so that we could be sure to stay in touch. E-mail was a passport to international friendship. Yes, a kind of modern miracle.

JUST ONE MORE
SATURDAY NIGHT

In Skillet it was raining, just as it had rained in every other town they had been to on the tour. Skillet boasted a deserted railway station hung with plastic bowls of dead geraniums, an empty market square littered with chip papers and empty drink cans, and a red-brick church surrounded by a treeless graveyard. As they walked into town Teresa counted six thrift shops, four fancy-goods shops, three supermarkets and three cafés. They were all shut. The rain beat down, streaking and darkening the grey concrete shopfronts. Teresa, Maggie and Damien plodded towards the public library, where their reading was being held. It was in the middle of a pedestrian precinct that was shutting up for the night as they arrived.

– Where's the nearest pub? Teresa asked half an hour later: I'd like a glass of wine before going on. A glass or two of red wine, that's what I always have.

The four of them were crammed into the tiny room above the public library that Gertrude called their green room. She had made this joke several times until they had acknowledged it with polite smiles. Now Gertrude frowned. She had been telling them all about regional arts policy and library reorganization in the area and Teresa had interrupted her detailed and complex description of her part-time job as assistant arts officer with special responsibility for literature events.

– The pubs here don't sell wine, she said: and in any case it's a pity to be dependent on alcohol in order to give a performance, isn't it? I'll ask the librarians if they've got some herb tea. I always have camomile. It's very soothing.

Damien snorted. He was lounging on a broken-backed office chair with his feet up on the rickety table, flicking through his books of poems and deciding what to read. He nodded at Gertrude as she swivelled her frown towards him, then indicated, with a lift of one eyebrow, his sports bag on the floor beside him. Teresa immediately realized it contained a bottle of whisky. Damien's right hand, sketching a quick outline in the air, told her that. He must have been to Skillet before, she thought. Maggie, washing her face in the deep square sink in the corner, snorted too. She spluttered through the soap and muffled her scorn in a towel.

– Personally, Gertrude said: I've never needed stimulants of any sort to help me express my creativity.

She tossed her head so that her gilt earrings clashed and jangled. She was tall and very thin, with a foxy face, small blue eyes, and pinched lips. She wore a long flowing black crêpe dress and several orange chiffon scarves. Her red hennaed hair dripped around her shoulders.

Maggie was backcombing her dyed blonde hair into a beehive. It kept nearly collapsing, soft as a new loaf. At last she got it into place and fixed it with spray and pins. She leaned forwards, clasping her bra together at the back, rolled on sheer black stockings and fastened them to her suspenders, then stepped into her ruched black nylon cocktail frock and wriggled it up over her thighs. Damien had been concentrating on his book, to give her an illusion of privacy while she changed. Now he looked up at her and winked.

– Crowded in here, isn't it? Maggie said to Teresa: do me up, darling, will you?

The librarians' cloakroom was also their kitchenette and storeroom. It smelt of old ashtrays and bleach, a whiff of urine from the lavatory next door, lavender air-freshener. Dusty cardboard boxes of books were piled against the walls. The frayed sage carpet was scarred with cigarette burns.

– It's nice to wear something pretty for poetry readings, isn't it? Gertrude cried, glancing at Teresa's tight lime-green satin trousers and low-cut, sleeveless black lace blouse: it's important to present a well-groomed image so that the audience can feel you've made a bit of an effort. We mustn't despise our audiences in the provinces!

– Are you reading tonight? Teresa asked: I thought there were just the three of us.

She jerked her head at the other two. Damien had taken his turn at the sink. He was squinting into the mirror that hung there, smoothing his eyebrows with a wetted forefinger and humming a little tune. Maggie perched on the table, her crossed legs showing white above her stocking-tops. She was buffing her nails and frowning.

– I'm the compère tonight, Gertrude explained: didn't anyone tell you? And in the first half we invite the local poets to read. Otherwise it's too élitist, just putting on established published poets. So the evening will start with Luke Gerison reading, he's a very well-known and well-respected local poet, and then myself of course, and then after a break, with tea and biscuits, you three. Ten minutes each, fifteen at a pinch, and please don't overrun your time.

Gertrude lit a cigarette and drew on it.

– Now, she said in an intimate and very kind voice, looking directly at Teresa: I expect you're feeling it's rather self-indulgent, rather pretentious, to read out your work to others and expect them to listen, believe me I understand, you must be wishing you could run away!

The acrid cigarette smoke was making Teresa's eyes water. She coughed loudly.

– So I thought I'd just run in and say hello and have a quick chat, Gertrude continued: and talk us all through what's expected of us. I'll keep my introductions very brief. It's important to avoid clichés, so I'll say very little, I don't want to load you with compliments and embarrass you. That would be false. I'll keep it simple.

– Wonderful, Maggie said, pouring whisky into the three cracked cups Damien had found in the metal cupboard behind the door: cheers, everybody.

– As a poet myself, Gertrude continued: I know so well how it feels to perform, I too get nervous, if you're at all sensitive you feel it's a crazy thing to do, isn't it, getting up on a stage and showing off in front of everybody as if the world owed you a living!

Teresa snapped shut the lid of her powder compact with a satisfyingly loud click. She sipped her whisky then sent Gertrude a lipsticked smile, full gloss.

– Who are your publishers? she asked.

Gertrude glared at her.

– Oh, I don't publish. Publishers these days, too stuffy and conventional to take me on. They prefer to play safe with safe writers. My work's too avant-garde for them.

She glanced at her watch.

– Heavens, is that the time? I must go downstairs and make sure the librarians have got everything ready.

She smiled reproachfully and trailed out.

Damien poured more whisky into their teacups.

– Break a leg, he said to Maggie and Teresa.

– Break a leg, they said back to him.

The evening began late. Gertrude stood at the library door, pinning up a notice to advertise the reading and saying she really ought to conquer her dislike of the media and do more publicity for these events. The poets helped the librarians put out the chairs, and the urn and teacups.

The audience arrived. Ten ladies from a writers group in a neighbouring town. They had got lost in the shopping precinct and had been trying to get in through the front door of the library, which of course was locked. For poetry readings, you had to come in through the back.

Luke Gerison strode in just as everybody was settling them-selves. He wore cowboy boots with silver spurs, and a Stetson. He had a bushy black moustache and flashing dark eyes. He stood with his hands on his hips while Gertrude drooped over the mike and wiped her hand across her brow.

Gertrude opened the evening by telling the audience how exhausted she was after compèring a very big literary festival the week before, up north. She explained that she couldn't think of any jokes to make, and mentioned the poets' names. She made a point of mentioning how nervous Teresa was and how well she was hiding it. Women of Teresa's age, she pointed out, did not nor-mally tour around the country with poets so much younger than themselves. She recognized that the ladies in the audience were women of roughly the same age as Teresa. They were bound to feel very shy. If they had questions to ask after the reading, they would probably prefer not to have to speak up in public, so they could write the questions on bits of paper and Gertrude would read them out on their behalf. Gertrude smiled wanly, flapped her hand, and sat down.

Luke Gerison leaped on to the tiny dais and began to read a poem about eternity. It went on for twenty minutes. Then Gertrude had her turn. She faced the audience. She declared: I *hate* war! Then she read a long anti-war poem. This too went on for twenty minutes. In between the verses were silences during which Gertrude glared at them. She seemed disappointed that they did not leap up and declare that they *loved* war.

– We're going to miss that last train if we're not careful, Teresa muttered to Maggie in the interval over a cup of lukewarm tea.

– It's gone already, Maggie said: Gertrude's just told me. She made a mistake. She got the times wrong. There *is* no late last train. She says we'll have to stay at one of the local pubs which does B and B.

The three of them performed in the second half for exactly ten minutes each. After the reading they shepherded the audience into the pub. The ten ladies quickly grew jolly and confiding. They told jokes and offered ribald stories and teased each other. They tossed back their gin. They had mini-cabs ordered to take them home, so they could have a few drinks, they explained to Teresa, and let their hair down.

Teresa went to the bar with Damien to organize a second round.

– Thanks, said Gertrude at her elbow: vodka and tonic please. A large one.

– What about our cheques? Teresa asked: I'd like mine now, if that's convenient.

– I don't hand out cheques just like that, Gertrude said in a shocked voice: please send me an invoice, in triplicate, and I'll pass it on to the finance office. I expect it will take a few weeks.

She shook her head at Teresa. She gazed reproachfully into her eyes.

– You don't need to express your insecurity this way. You were quite good, you know. I was really pleasantly surprised. I think you have some real talent there!

A hand spread itself on the small of Teresa's back, clamped her spine. The old beer and bad-breath smell belonged to Luke Gerison. He gave her a closeup of his rumpled and reddened skin.

– Baby, he growled: those poems you read, they were passionate poems, erotic poems, you know?

– Mmmm, Teresa said.

She sipped her red wine. The pub had turned out to sell it after all. It was thick and sweet, like cough medicine.

– You didn't read them right, Luke said: like, your performance could of been so much more erotic, know what I mean? You should of read them in a really sexy way.

He moved his hand to and fro across her shoulder-blades and yelled above the juke-box.

– Baby, you shouldn't be so uptight when you read erotic poems like that. You should practise some more. I could show you how. I really dig older women. You've got to feel it, deep down here inside.

Teresa flinched away, her hands full of drinks.

– Please show Gertrude, she said: I know you have so much to give but I'm busy just now.

She nodded her head in the direction of the ten ladies, a vivacious and pink-cheeked group squashed around a corner table. Later on, at closing-time, Gertrude sped away with Luke in his Ford Sierra.

– Goodbye, Gertrude, Maggie said: normally I never forget a name or a face, but I'll make an exception in your case.

They dined on potato crisps, then crept upstairs, to their bedrooms that smelt of beer and cigarettes. Teresa lay on the orange chenille bedspread and began to laugh. Well, old girl, she said to herself: you're not doing too badly. Fifty-two years old and you're still on the road. At least you're still getting the gigs.

She knew she wouldn't sleep. The nylon-mix easy-care sheets could be rejected. The milk train was at five. She could be on it. She left a note for the publican, telling him to send the bill to Gertrude, and crept out. At five a.m. she jumped on to the train. Two hours later, she was walking down her own street, hopping over dog turds and composing a poem. A performance poem, a sort of middle-aged rap. She sang it out loud, joyfully. She'd been on tour earning her living and now she was going home to Ned. She stopped in front of their shabby house. The curtains were drawn. She'd creep in. She'd tiptoe up the stairs. She'd slide into bed and his arms would close round her and hold her tight.

A Story for Hallowe'en

It began with the voices, the sound of muttering that pressed up against the back of her neck, as though the voices were hands that grasped and stroked her, raising gooseflesh. After a little, the voices ceased quarrelling and sank away to a whisper, to be replaced by an unnerving solo, a thin, high, wavering humming that went on and on, until Clothilde sat up in the darkness and cried out and the unearthly humming stopped.

She knew that the farmhouse was supposedly haunted. The notary who showed them the place and sold it to them mentioned, with a sniff, something about peasant prejudices. Their new neighbours further up the hill recounted the tale with relish over glasses of kir and dishes of salted crackers. The postman advised Clothilde to put a statue of the Virgin in the empty niche over the front door, as protection. The lady in the bakery cocked her head every morning when they went in for the bread, as though waiting to hear news of hideous apparitions.

Clothilde and Fernande repeated to everyone who offered them these rumours, these hints and shrugs and winks: We don't believe in ghosts.

Of course the house had character, or, as Fernande put it: atmosphere. She was the more romantic one, with a nose for such things. She had fallen in love with the house at first sight, a jumble of tumbledown buildings around a courtyard, set in isolation half-way up the hill outside the village of Sainte-Gemme-les-Fleuves, backed by woods and looped about with streams and tiny waterfalls. While the notary conscientiously pointed out the collapsed walls, the holes in the roof, the faulty wiring, the lack of septic tank, the dilapidation of barns and out-houses, and the possibility of ghosts, Fernande imagined the vine spreadeagled against the back wall, the brimming vegetable plot edged with pinks and daisies, the kitchen full of their friends feasting and carousing. She sat on the doorstep, looking out of the courtyard, down the lane into the little valley spread with corn-fields and orchards. She said to Clothilde who was inspecting the cracked metal lid of the well in the centre of the courtyard: I insist you buy this house.

The notary explained that, centuries before, the farmhouse had been part of a small convent. The name of the house – Terredieu, God's earth – confirmed that. Nuns had sung the Divine Office in what was now the cowshed. Clothilde and Fernande picked their way through the mud into the manure-scented darkness, across a rough floor of combed concrete littered with straw and ancient cowpats. The notary showed them the ramshackle tower at the back of the house, called the oubliette, in which disobedient nuns would have been locked up on a diet of bread and water. He showed them the dormitory upstairs, where the nuns had once slept, now a grain store, its corners silted with corn husks. He pointed out traces of the original cloister around the courtyard. Flinching, he opened the door of the outside privy and let them peer in. Finally, with a contemptuous smile, he mentioned the local people's belief that the house was haunted.

– Oh do tell us the story, Fernande begged, ignoring Clothilde's frown.

The notary shrugged.

– These stupid peasants will believe anything. It's the usual: a nun having a love affair, discovered to be pregnant, so locked up in the oubliette. The prioress set her to sewing shrouds as a punishment. She sewed one for herself and one for the baby. In her sixth month of pregnancy she killed herself and the unborn child. She knotted the shrouds together and hung herself from a hook in the ceiling.

Clothilde was quite pale, her face glistening with sweat. She said loudly: Fernande and I do not believe in ghosts.

Later on the postman amplified the story.

– It was a double sin, you see. First of all the sin against purity, and then suicide, which is the great sin, the sin against the Holy Ghost. So no wonder her spirit can't rest. She is probably in hell. But if she is in purgatory, she's got a chance of getting to heaven one day. Of course all the souls in purgatory need our prayers.

The neighbours up the hill, Parisian cultural historians enjoying their second home at weekends and enchanted by the quaint folk-lore of the district, added their own flourish to the tale.

– People say she walks on the night of the full moon, every month, wearing her shroud. You have to bar all the doors and windows against her, so that she can't get in.

Fernande sighed with relish, curling her long hands, with their red fingernails, around her glass of kir, and admiring her gold ring with its big green tourmaline, which Clothilde had given her for her birthday the previous week.

Clothilde snapped: as a pharmacist with a rigorous scientific training I can tell you that ghosts do not exist, except in the im-agination of neurotic people probably in need of anti-depressants.

Her round face was as pink as her silk trouser suit. Fernande changed the subject and began to explain how Clothilde had sold her pharmacy in Le Mans to buy the house here in Saint-Gemme, and how she planned to work as a locum in the district.

– And you, Madame? enquired the neighbours, smiles of curios-ity flickering across their faces: will you live here all the time too? You write children's books, you said. Will you be able to do your writing here?

– Oh, we'll see, Fernande said, laughing.

The lady in the bakery added the final flourish.

– The previous owner of the house lives in Alençon, as you probably know, of course. For a long time she let it out to the tenant farmers who were living in it previously. They brought up six children there. Then she evicted them, because she thought she'd like to do up the place to use as a holiday home. But after just one month in the house, organizing all the local builders and so on to come in and give her estimates for the work, she changed her mind and put the house on the market. She wanted to get rid of it as fast as she could.

– Perhaps she had a guilty conscience, Fernande suggested: getting rid of her tenants like that, it sounds rather brutal.

The woman behind the counter lifted two baguettes from the rack and handed them over the counter.

– Oh, they don't mind. They were due to retire, in any case. They've got a brand-new bungalow three kilometres away, near all their children, they're content. They say a modern house with all mod cons is so much pleasanter. And no ghost. Can you imagine – they saw the ghost six times.

She nodded at Fernande.

– We're all pleased to see the house being properly lived in again.

She counted out Fernande's change.

– We are tolerant people, she said, not meeting her customer's eyes: we respect one another, you'll find we are all friends here, in the country. We don't make problems for each other.

Clothilde, who was waiting outside in the car, smiled when these words were recounted to her.

– We must make sure to give them something to talk about, in that case.

The local people watched the two women settle in to Terredieu. Carloads of visitors were seen to come and go, vans full of furniture drove up, workmen were summoned to dig the septic tank, mend the roof, brace the walls, fix the wiring, install a bathroom. Autumn arrived. Clothilde climbed ladders to clear gutters and mend shutters and replace panes of glass. She was fortifying the house against the approach of winter. In her red jeans and heavy boots she was a sturdy, cheerful figure. She was clearly the masculine one of the queer couple, the villagers decided. They had it all worked out. Fernande, who was more often seen in a skirt, raking the orchard and weeding the gravel, was obviously the feminine one.

– In your hearing, the cultural historians explained: they'll be as polite as you like. But behind your backs they'll call you horrible names.

In October, in their sixth month in the house, on the night of the full moon, Clothilde was woken by the sound of voices. Two women muttering. Protesting. Having a quarrel. She sat up. Moonlight drove between the curtains and whitened the wooden floor. The voices ricocheted across the stripes of moonlight.

– You don't really want to, do you?

– But I do want to, so much.

Fernande was fast asleep beside her. Clothilde jumped out of bed. She fastened the curtains together with safety-pins, so that not a crack opened for the moon to pour streams of silver through. She trembled. The voices fingered the back of her neck and brought her out in goose bumps. She dived back under the duvet, pulled it round her shoulders, buried her face in Fernande's sleeping back, stuck her fingers in her ears. She could not understand why she was alarmed. She repeated to herself: I am a pharmacist with a rigorous training in science, I do not believe in ghosts. She thought: I had a glass too many of wine at dinner, it's upset my digestion, that's all. I'm imagining things.

She took her fingers out of her ears, and tried to relax.

Then the humming began. A high-pitched lonely voice shaking itself into the air, a tuneless, eerie sound that went on and on until Clothilde sat up in the darkness, pressed her hands to her cheeks, and whimpered. The room vibrated as the humming ceased. Fernande slept on. Now the silence felt threatening. Fear drove Clothilde out of bed again, over to the door. She gripped the wooden latch in both hands, feeling sick. For some reason she was assuming it was locked, but it wasn't. She went next door to the bathroom, and threw up.

In the morning Fernande exclaimed with concern at Clothilde's pale face, at the dark rings under her eyes, at her shaking hands as she tried to spread apricot jam on a piece of bread.

– I'm all right, Clothilde snapped: I think I'm coming down with a cold, that's all. I didn't sleep too well last night.

Fernande drained her cup of coffee. She yawned and stretched like someone who has slept extremely well. She sounded horribly cheerful.

– You're not working today, are you? So why not go back to bed for a bit? Take some aspirin and catch up on some sleep. I'll go into the village and do the shopping. Have a rest.

Clothilde had a bath and put on a clean nightdress. She changed the sheets on the bed, not wanting to return to the sweat of last night's terror. She lay back against the pillows. She heard the skitter of gravel as Fernande's Deux Chevaux sped away.

Now the house was hushed and calm. Clothilde was dozing, a river of images slipping past in a play of light, floating under the soft cotton of the duvet cover smelling of ironing. The clean pillowcase was cool against her cheek. She was swirling down towards deep sleep.

She was remembering that today was the Feast of All Souls, the eve of the Feast of All Saints. A day of transition. The day when, as a child, she had always gone with schoolfriends into church to pray for the souls of the dead who were reputed to wander abroad on this day begging for the prayers of the living so that they might be released finally from the fires of purgatory into the bright joys of heaven. The more churches you visited on All Souls Day, the children were taught, the more souls you liberated from purgatory.

The humming began. Insistent, pricking at Clothilde's eyelids. High and thin, pitched between a tune and a mindless chant. It was the humming sound a person makes to accompany her sewing. When you have the long hems of a shroud to stitch, you hum to keep your fingers steadily moving along. Clothilde thought: the ghost has got in, she has got inside somehow. Her fingers, clutched together under the sheet, were lumps of ice. Shivers pushed up and down her back, making her gulp. She opened her eyes.

A young woman, heavily pregnant, sat cross-legged on the floor, her profile bent over the baby's long robe to whose hem she was tacking a deep frill of lace. She hummed a high song as she drove her needle in and out. When she lifted her head to meet Clothilde's eyes she smiled. She winked. Then she vanished.

Now, at last, Clothilde understood what all this was about.

– I want a child, she explained to Fernande over lunch: I want us to have a baby and become parents.

– You don't really want to, do you? Fernande stammered.

– Oh but I do, Clothilde said: so much.

Now it was Fernande's turn to become the practical one, while Clothilde dreamed.

Fernande thought for quite a while. Then she laid her plans accordingly. She explained to Clothilde what she had decided they should do. They would have to be very discreet, to avoid causing gossip, and they must operate separately.

They had assumed that only one of them would become pregnant. They had agreed that whoever became pregnant first, well, she would be the one to give birth to the baby. But in fact they both conceived at around the same time. Their babies were born within a few weeks of each other, and baptized together at the village church, wearing the long frilled christening robes that Clothilde had stitched during the months of waiting. The two cultural historians acted as godparents.

The villagers, crowding into the village hall after the ceremony for the *vin d'honneur*, were politely congratulatory, as was proper, but also puzzled. After all their speculation, it seemed that the two *gouines* were not *gouines* at all. Merely immoral and promiscuous. Nobody could be quite sure. The postman and the notary both had their own reasons for believing the two women to be cured of their lesbianism, by virtue of their seducers' astonishing sexual prowess, but, chivalrous to the last, and not wanting to get into trouble with their wives, they simply stroked their noses and smiled mysteriously and kept this knowledge to themselves.

MA SEMBLABLE
MA SOEUR

for Margi Defriez

Once upon a time, quite recently, there were two sisters. Twins. Not identical, although they were very alike, with curly brown hair and wide mouths. Lily had hazel eyes and Rose bluey-green ones. To help out the teachers at school, who were not always sure of distinguishing between them correctly, they had their names embroidered on the breast pockets of their pink gingham frocks in flowing chain stitch. They thought this was ridiculous. Wasn't it obvious that Lily was Lily and Rose was Rose? Their parents, of course, and their friends, always knew which was which. Lily was the adventurous one, thinking up new games and dares, playing football and cricket with the boys' gang in the street, while Rose sat in the back garden and dressed and undressed her dolls, or read. They shared a bedroom, and at night Rose would whisper stories across the gap in between their twin beds. Finally her voice would tail off and they would both fall asleep.

They loitered through secondary school together, sitting side by side at the back of the class, helping each other out with homework when necessary. They did just enough revision to pass their exams and spent as much time as possible enjoying themselves. They dawdled in coffee bars sipping cappuccino from smoky glass cups, or went bowling, or lolled in the back row of the cinema, or practised their jiving skills at the local youth club. They often teamed up as a foursome with the boyfriends of the moment. Being much the same size they could swap clothes and so double their wardrobes. Lily could lend Rose her new turquoise mohair skirt and borrow her winklepickers in return. On weekend nights they backcombed their hair into frizzy beehives, rolled on glinting bronze nylons, and hit the town. The world was theirs, and they were in the world together, and they were complete.

When they were twenty this companionship changed. Rose, who had been working as a secretary, got married, and accompanied her husband to the village in the countryside where he worked as a painter and decorator. Lily moved to the city, where she got a job as a photographer's assistant. They began to see less of each other.

Not that they'd become estranged, exactly. More that they needed to become independent now that they were grown-up and living adult lives. Twin girls could happily nest in each other's pockets, but modern women had their own homes to go to. Not to mention families. Tending a man, three children, a house and a garden kept Rose busy. There was always another pile of laundry to iron, another sinkful of washing-up to do, another floor to mop. Money was tight, so she got a part-time job as soon as all the children were old enough to attend the village school, as a dinner lady in the school kitchen. She was a good cook, who enjoyed giving people delicious things to eat. She knew how to make the sort of healthy meals that the parents approved of and that the pupils would actually consume with gusto.

She had two philosophies as a chef. One was: a little bit of what you fancy does you good. The other was: when in doubt, overdo it. People liked coming to dinner with Rose and her husband, because they could look forward to good food and plenty of it. Second helpings offered as a matter of course. Rose became plump but she did not care. She felt it was sensual. All the women she knew were on diets, except for Lily who was almost as skinny as a boy. After coming to dinner at her house Rose's neighbours would starve themselves the following day. In defiance of their cardboard crispbreads and low-fat margarines tasting of axle grease Rose would pour an additional measure of extra virgin olive oil on to her spaghetti and eat twice as much as she had intended.

What of Lily meanwhile? Her life was very different from her sister's. Her driving ambition was to become a successful photographer. To achieve this aim she worked in a series of badly paid jobs. At the beginning of her career she was the studio dogsbody, the one who handed the cameras and changed the lenses and adjusted the lights. She learned by watching others. She did a course at college in her early thirties and decided to specialize in portraits. Behind the camera she was discreet, kind and funny. People liked having their photo taken by her because she put them at their ease and stopped them worrying about not being good-looking enough. Besides freelancing, she did wedding and christening pictures for her friends.

Lily did not want to marry or to have children. How could you possibly remain faithful to one man all your life? she thought. These days we all live too long. She preferred to take a succession of lovers instead, to have a string of love affairs. Some of these were disastrous, some less so. Once the men discovered that Lily was not the domestic sort, which sooner or later even the most bohemian of them turned out to want, they drifted off and married someone else.

Lily was scared by Rose's life. Non-stop toiling for others, with no time for herself. Oh, she could see the satisfactions, the fulfilments involved, in bearing and raising three good-tempered well-behaved girls, as Rose had done. She passionately envied her, from time to time, her handsome husband, her solid home. But whenever the opportunity presented itself to Lily of settling down and getting pregnant she did not take it. Rose has done it for both of us, she used to say: we don't both need to become mothers. And you can't have it all, I know that, I'm not one of your romantic idealists, oh no, I've made my choice and I'm happy with it.

People shook their heads over Lily and called her selfish and immature. As the years passed they began to remark that it was just as well she had not had children. She would have made a terrible mother. As well as being so self-obsessed, she smoked far too much, and she was dreadfully thin. She never wore anything but jeans and a black leather jacket and she drove an MG. No wonder men were frightened of her.

She and Rose lived so far apart that they hardly ever saw each other. They talked regularly on the phone. Rose could not be bothered to go up to town, much as she loved Lily. Once the children had left home to attend college, she had become a passionate gardener as well as cook, turning her back garden into a *potager* and also acquiring an allotment. Round the edges of both she grew flowers: old-fashioned, highly scented roses, pastel drifts of annuals sown in different patterns every year. She won prizes for her dahlias at the village show. She experimented with different kinds of clematis and honeysuckle. She made room for a small wild-flower meadow, a knot of herbs, a parterre.

Gardening took up a great deal of her time, like a lover. When she was made redundant from her job as school cook, she started a small business, supplying the local restaurants with organic produce and cut blooms for tables. She wore old clothes nearly all the time, so that she could nip into the garden at a moment's notice and put in half an hour's digging. Her fingernails were permanently clotted with earth. She tied her hair back with a piece of twine. She stomped about in wellington boots and was extremely happy. She loved her husband as dearly as ever but she forgot about him for days on end, assuming that he was as busy and content as she.

It came as an enormous shock to Rose, therefore, when her husband told her that he was having an affair with the local GP's receptionist, a blue-eyed blonde thirty years younger than he was, and that he wanted a trial separation. Rose, he pointed out, had been neglecting herself lately. She had been neglecting her appearance, her figure and him. They hadn't had sex for two months. What was a man to do? He was off.

He did not go very far. He moved into a room above the butcher's, which he furnished with a large futon and a bedside lamp with a pink shade. His new place was a bedsit really but he called it a studio flat. Here he could receive the receptionist, who still lived at home.

– And the worst of it, Rose wailed over the phone to Lily: is that everybody in the village has known about it for weeks. They saw them drinking in the pub at lunchtime and drew their own conclusions. I suppose he must have wanted everybody to know, otherwise he wouldn't have gone to the local. And that wretched girl! I used to serve her school dinners not so long ago. She used to love my treacle tart. Now I wish I'd poisoned her.

She sobbed loudly.

– Everybody knew about it. Except for me.

– Jump into a cab, Lily instructed her: go straight to the station and get a ticket up to town. Come and stay with me for a bit. You need to get away.

– I suppose I could take the weekend off, Rose said: though I hate leaving the garden.

– The garden will manage without you, Lily said: unlike your marriage. Do you want to save your marriage or not?

– I suppose so, Rose said: we certainly used to have lovely sex. When we got around to it.

– Lucky you, Lily said.

Rose sorted through her clothes, trying to find a few outfits suitable for wear in town. She decided that she would have to go shopping with Lily and buy herself something nice. Fashionable, flattering and sexy was what she meant. At the moment her wardrobe mainly consisted of large, ancient pairs of shorts and trousers and faded T-shirts, plus a sou'wester and a 1940s men's tweed coat she had bought twenty years ago and worn ever since.

Her one frock, a sort of shepherdess smock in flowered purple with
a lace collar, purchased at Laura Ashley in the mid-sixties, was not,
she decided, really becoming. She stuffed all these garments back
into the cupboard and travelled up to town in her one classic item
of clothing, the multi-purpose suit, a black wool outfit she mostly
wore for village funerals. The skirt no longer did up at the waist so
she fastened it with a safety-pin.

Lily met her off the train.

– Darling darling, she said, embracing her: oh I've missed you
so much.

There began for them now a kind of honeymoon, in which they
returned to being girls together again. Lily took a week's holiday
from work and persuaded Rose to do the same. Rose phoned up
her main restaurant clients and instructed them to help themselves to any herbs, flowers and vegetables they wanted from the
potager. She would send them the bill on her return. Then she
relaxed into just being with Lily.

They went out for lunch, they dawdled on café pavements drinking aperitifs, they both had their greying hair cut and coloured, they
bought new clothes to go with the golden and terracotta streaks
now subtly highlighting their brown curls. They lay on Lily's big
double bed for hours at a time, gossiping, painting their toenails,
reading novels, listening to music, watching videos and eating take-
aways. They talked about their work. Lily showed Rose how to use
a camera. Rose dragged Lily around the city parks and told her the
names of all the plants. Sometimes they went clubbing, to those
clubs where middle-aged women were tolerated. On these occasions
they amused themselves by dressing in identical get-ups. Lily had

gained weight with all the lying around on beds grazing on delicious snacks, while Rose had shed some pounds with all the walking around shopping, and so, for the first time in many years, they looked alike again, like the twins they actually were.

They said goodbye to one another very affectionately, and swore it would not be long before they met again.

Rose's husband came back to the house with a bag of washing, for there was no launderette in the village. He was astonished to find his wife, clad in a curvy pair of black leather trousers and a skimpy chiffon vest, painting her toenails in the kitchen. She smiled sexily at him. They spent the rest of the afternoon making passionate love.

I'd forgotten what a marvellous colour your hair is, Rose's husband told her: oh my darling, forgive me, I've been such a fool. Why on earth did I ever want to leave you?

Meanwhile, in town, Lily was developing a new, naïve style of photography. People had grown tired of too much sophistication. Lily's almost childish portraits made a welcome change. The number of her clients increased. Her social life flourished too, for as she had put on weight so also she seemed to have gained in humour and charm. People queued up to take her out to dinner and the theatre. Men kept proposing marriage to her and she had a lovely time refusing them all.

The twins decided to continue like this. Every couple of months or so they swapped lives again, so that each could enjoy what she'd previously missed, and so they carried on happily ever after having the best of both worlds.

IN MY SHOES

As soon as I spotted those wedge-heeled fur mules I wanted them. But would the shop stock them in my size?

All through my adolescence the most desirable shoes were always too small for me to jam on. Or else, if I bought them, ignoring the warmth inflaming suddenly tender heels, the pinched and cramped toes, the tension that warned of trouble to come, and hobbled home in them, knees clenched, from the shops, they'd rub me sore until I limped, my flesh blistered and raw, or else I yanked the spiked things off and walked the last mile barefoot, and either way the hot wrinkled skin split and turned to blood, and I ended up feeling like the girl dancing in merciless red slippers for all eternity, and then had to spend the evening lancing tight fat cushions of water with darning needles and applying strips of pink Elastoplast fore and aft before lying with my throbbing feet propped on the sofa arm and swearing that never again would I let shoes break me in. The easier thing would have been to saw off my toes with a razor blade and shave my heels, as Cinderella's two sisters did.

That was back in the mid-1960s, when teenagers had only recently been invented, and the range of suitable footwear was still limited. Winklepickers and stilettos defined the feet of the dainty heroine. Up to size six was just about all right, size seven was pushing your luck, but size eight was freakish. I had long strong toes, the first three all of the same length, perfect for ballerinas going up on point. But I was not a ballerina because I was five foot seven. Over five foot six and you were out of the ballet class, your blocked shoes, bloodstained, tossed into the bin.

The lady in Freeman Hardy & Willis who X-rayed our feet at the start of every school term, and let us peer down the eyepiece of her chestnut plastic machine at our waggle of bones, pursed her lips. Her mute whistle spelled out healthy but huge. Propping my foot on a slope-sided stool, heel cupped on a leather-padded plywood curve, flesh braced between sliding metal calipers that measured width and length, the cold metal exciting me even as it confined, she confirmed that for me only one model of school indoor shoe was available, flat and brown and floppy, with leather tassels on leather ties. My friends experimented with black patent for Saturday nights but I partnered those indefatigable school shoes to ballroom lessons and parties and youth-club dances and they remained faithful to me and never wore out. I wanted flash chrome buckles, crêpe-soled brothel creepers, green suede, Chelsea boots, calf-hugging Courrèges white plastic with gilt zips, but they didn't fit.

– Your feet are nearly as big as mine, laughed jolly Uncle Dick one Boxing Day, hugging me then lining up his sheepskin-edged red and cream tartan slipper against my serviceable boat: what a lovely big girl you're getting to be.

The shoes of priests gleamed black and serious as saloon cars. The nuns wore black laceups over grey woollen stockings. We pupils were besandalled pilgrims soldiering up the mountain away from the grime and shame of girlhood towards purity.

In the late sixties I went barefoot over city pavements, enjoying the cool roughness of stone and the disgusted looks of passers-by. Filthy hippie treading in dogshit and sneaking smears of it back into college to pollute the atmosphere.

The early 1970s meant carnival. I joined a street theatre group and tried on garish costumes. These days feet were meant to look large, swollen and propped on monstrous platforms very like the pattens John Evelyn described the Venetian courtesans wearing in the seventeenth century, shoes so absurdly high that a lady needed to be handed about her business by a couple of swains, one on each side. Shoes that lifted you high above puddles and mess. I tittuped on and off buses in apple-green platforms with four-inch soles and a puckered green ankle strap. I tottered, a clown on stilts.

In the late 1970s I experimented with different disguises, cutting off all my hair and enjoying annoying Uncle Dick who repeated that I was very ugly. To go on demonstrations and to attend political meetings I wore heavy laced boots, the precursors of Doc Martens. When I went out dancing I wore a padded flying suit and gold high-heeled sandals. Or a ballgown with wellingtons. I used to be such a nice girl but not anymore.

I married my husband, an arts journalist, mainly because he admired my feet. My claims to beauty were modest. I did have slender ankles. Now he pointed to my high arches, my general neatness and narrowness, my long fine straight toes. We lived in Florence for a while. I coveted Italian shoes, which are better cut than shoes of any other nationality. I conquered my bashfulness, and went shopping. The saleswoman stooped over me. I whispered the size I needed.

– *Quarante-due per la signora*, she hollered.

Passers-by clattered in off the street to regard the giantess, and collided in the doorway with bemused shop assistants. Between them, the eager women found me a pair of flat green satin sling-backs, on a thick black rubber sole, held on by a wide strip of black elastic. Shoes that made me feel skittish and pretty, and that I wore until they rotted. But my marriage did not last. My habit of not wearing slippers let me down. I explained that slippers reminded me of Uncle Dick, but my husband was more concerned with the nasty diseases or verrucas one might pick up, if one went barefoot over Italian marble floors. It was so difficult to spot if the speckled tiles were dirty or clean.

Thirteen years on I like my feet because at last I can find plenty of shoes that fit. I can walk to parties in trainers, swinging my shoebag, and slip on my fake-crocodile heels at the door.

Uncle Dick died not long ago. To his funeral I wore a pair of high, wedge-heeled mules covered in sleek fur. You could run in them, if you needed to.

HYPSIPYLE TO JASON

for Jim Latter

You've gone. You left four days ago, at nine in the morning, speeding off in the little blue MG. A kiss, a wave, a toot on the horn, and you shot away.

I watched you vanish out of sight around the bend in the lane then came back into the empty house which suddenly felt much bigger. It isn't empty of course. But I've had to discover a new relationship to the space which is your absence. I've forgotten what unbroken solitude, day in, day out, is like. I'm no longer used to living on my own. All day long we work in our separate studios, not seeing anyone, not talking, as though we're on two different islands, and then at night we throw rope bridges across; we're together. Last night I was woken by an owl hooting outside, and reached for you, and you weren't there. The bed felt too wide, even though I'd filled it with pillows.

While you're away I listen to the silence. I discover that the silence here is full of sounds. Sitting on the front step, cradling a glass of red wine, I can hear the rasp of invisible crickets, the thrumming of bees sucking at the geraniums, the skitter of lizards dashing from rock to rock. I distinguish the song of different birds, from the cawing of rooks to the cooing of wood pigeons to the squabbles of chaffinches, blackbirds and bluetits over the nuts and bread I've put out for them. Jays and magpies whirr through the orchard. Sparrows zip past my ear, showing off the tight neat circuits of their flight, dart round the pines at the side of the house once or twice, then shave back past my cheek again. The wren nesting just above the doorframe does the same when I go in or out, just to show me who's boss. A dark streaking whistle of wings and she vanishes. Then a moment or two later I spot her hopping along the path under the honeysuckle arch, sidling back towards the door to reclaim her territory.

Aeroplanes dawdle across overhead in the afternoons. A sound of summer I remember from childhood. Lounging outside, sprawled on the grass, and hearing planes go by, high up. Machinery weaves in another constant thread of gentle noise. This time of year the tractors are out till late at night. Sometimes I hear them coming home at nearly dawn. With rain threatened, the harvest must be got in as fast as possible. The rain won't wait and nor must the corn.

In the meadows surrounding the house the cows and bullocks chew grass noisily with slapping jaws. Sometimes they low and bellow at each other across the dividing hedges, suddenly get frisky and thump up and down their pastures. You can hear their hoofs beating the ground. At six o'clock every evening a deep hum rises as the milking machines are switched on in our neighbours' farms. You can't see most of them behind the gentle hills enclosing our tiny valley, but you hear their vehicles trundle along the road that joins the bottom of our lane, their dogs bark on the other side of the forest. You hear the women hullooing at the geese, rounding up the turkeys and ducks and chickens at night, driving them into their sheds.

The silence is made up of all these sounds, and it's also a geography which opens up around me and under my feet. A new country which now I must explore.

Your absence means no one telling me ridiculous jokes or clowning to make me laugh, recounting anecdotes about your day in the studio and tales of your childhood and sudden memories of your earlier life which just pop up on to your tongue, no one putting on silly voices, doing imitations, singing exaggerated loud snatches of pop songs or old-time music hall, teasing me, inventing nonsense words and crazy rhymes which you recite out loud, calling for me in elaborate imitation birdsong, dropping things and cursing, thwacking the axe on to logs of wood, walking around warbling and whistling upstairs as you run your bath while I sit by the fire, playing jazz very loud while I get the supper on.

Your voice my music. I listen for you. When you've been out doing the shopping I hear you coming home when you're still miles away, my ears are attuned to you, there's a slight alteration in the silence which is you changing gear and then five minutes later you arrive, charging up the slope to the house, pull up outside the back door, scattering gravel. Over supper, by candlelight, you tell me your secrets. In the bath, reclining opposite me, you lift your foot and stroke the curly blonde hair on my cunt with your toes. The golden fleece. In the night, in the darkness, you whisper to me words of love as you hold me in your arms.

Now, while you're not here, while you're far away, I hear your voice all the time, whether I'm working indoors or digging the vegetable garden or lounging on the front step watching the evening light go pink on the roof of the farmhouse across the valley.

So don't come back just yet. Stay away just a little while longer.

Let me enjoy delay and lack and have a honeymoon of not having you. Give me the time to miss you more, to relish that, to feel even more lonely. Desperately to long for your return. To wait impatiently by the open door hours before you're due. To walk about in this full, roomy solitude and this resonant silence, to compose this letter, my ship that sails to you, my freight, my spell magically conjuring your presence on paper, imagining what we will do and say on your return, words I shall not need to write down and send to you because you will have come back, you will be here with me and I'll never despatch this letter but tear it up into bits and scatter it, white fragments falling silently like our clothes on to the floor.

Also by Michèle Roberts

FAIR EXCHANGE

'Her characters inhabit the moment expansively, and are rounded out with Roberts' characteristic humour and sensuousness' *Times*

Drawing on the secrets and affairs of two of the most famous and passionate figures of the late 19th century – Mary Wollstonecraft and William Wordsworth – this book is written in beautiful, beguiling prose.

In the early 1800s, Louise, a French peasant, fearing she is about to die, calls for her priest. She has a secret to confess. Though the priest is impatient, she wants to tell her tale from the beginning. It opens in London in the 1780s, when Jemima Boote arrives at Mary Wollstonecraft's school. Later she follows her beloved teacher to Paris, wanting to be part of the erupting revolution, and then – six months pregnant – retreats to the village of Louise's youth. Her arrival coincides with that of another young mother-to-be, Annette, who has been sent by her parents to the country to hide her disgraceful pregnancy and to get over her infatuation with William, a young English poet. In an abandoned convent they take up waiting: waiting for their babies, waiting for their men.

IMPOSSIBLE SAINTS

'*Impossible Saints*, like the life of a real saint, is dangerously close to perfection' Kate Saunders, *Independent*

'Her fictions are high-risk, unconventional, often apparently unstable, yet are steered with such authority that the otherwise cautious reader is taken almost without realising it into dangerous and exhilarating territory . . . She is a writer dedicated to challenging the boundaries by which the idle and unthinking might try to circumscribe her' Rachel Cusk, *Sunday Express*

Always bold, always provocative, Michèle Roberts turns to the forbidden pleasures and pains of the love between father and daughter and unfolds before us the life and death of Saint Josephine. Like beads in a rosary, the heady tales of other 'impossible' female saints – one-armed mad girls, beauties locked in towers, seductive daughters – are woven throughout her beguiling and passionate story.

Now you can order superb titles directly from Virago

☐	Flesh and Blood	Michèle Roberts	£6.99
☐	Impossible Saints	Michèle Roberts	£6.99
☐	All the Selves I Was	Michèle Roberts	£8.99
☐	During Mother's Absence	Michèle Roberts	£5.99
☐	Food, Sex & God	Michèle Roberts	£9.99
☐	Daughters of the House	Michèle Roberts	£6.99

Please allow for postage and packing: **Free UK delivery**.
Europe: add 25% of retail price; Rest of World: 45% of retail price.

To order any of the above or any other Virago titles, please call our credit card orderline or fill in this coupon and send/fax it to:

Virago, 250 Western Avenue, London, W3 6XZ, UK.
Fax 020 8324 5678   Telephone 020 8324 5516

☐ I enclose a UK bank cheque made payable to Virago for £
☐ Please charge £ . . . . to my Access, Visa, Delta, Switch Card No.

Expiry Date ☐☐☐☐   Switch Issue No. ☐☐

NAME (Block letters please) . . . .

ADDRESS . . . .

Postcode . . . . Telephone . . . .

Signature . . . .

Please allow 28 days for delivery within the UK. Offer subject to price and availability.

Please do not send any further mailings from companies carefully selected by Virago ☐